George Bassett

Hippolyte and Golden-beak : two stories

George Bassett

Hippolyte and Golden-beak : two stories

ISBN/EAN: 9783743322141

Manufactured in Europe, USA, Canada, Australia, Japa

Cover: Foto ©Andreas Hilbeck / pixelio.de

Manufactured and distributed by brebook publishing software
(www.brebook.com)

George Bassett

Hippolyte and Golden-beak : two stories

"LEDYARD WAS TRYING TO PERSUADE HER TO LEAVE THE TABLE"

HIPPOLYTE

AND

GOLDEN-BEAK

Two Stories

BY

GEORGE BASSETT

ILLUSTRATED

NEW YORK
HARPER & BROTHERS PUBLISHERS
1895

CONTENTS

ILLUSTRATIONS

MR. JAMES McNEILL WHISTLER:

To you, *cher Maître*, who knew Hippolyte in the flesh, I send this little portrait — to you whose brush renders your friends immortal, and whose pen reduces to their last mortality the enemies it is your gentle art to make perceptible. For us, who have only black and white upon our palettes, it remains to link our wagons to your star as best we can.

It is a far cast to darkened Chelsea and the bright garden of the rue du Bac from the lake-gemmed forests of Wisconsin in whose shades I made these pages. But Rajon's picture of your face is pinned upon my canvas wall, and to those who love you the little miles and the little months seem very short.

G. B.

Lake Tired-Canoe, *September*, 1893.

HIPPOLYTE

I

IT was in Paris that I found the valet
with whom this little narrative concerns itself—found him there and lost him there;
and all so recently that it is almost an indelicacy to talk about him.   I had told the
maître d'hôtel of my club that I was looking for a servant, and he permitted himself
to entertain the hope that he might assist
monsieur in his search.

"It is only a boy," he said, "but he is a
boy with a long head.   It is my nephew,
monsieur, and my poor brother has not
been happy this year.   They are working
jewellers in the Faubourg St. Denis, and,
what with all the cheap trinkets stamped
out by the machine these days, there isn't

enough work to keep the lad busy at home,
and he must find some other trade. He's a
good boy, monsieur, and if you try him you
will find I'm not wrong when I say he has
an old head on young shoulders. But I
can't give him a place here in the club.
Monsieur can understand that I couldn't
do right by him. I'd have to be harder
with him than with any of the other pages,
or there 'd be fusses every night."

Now I had a great respect for the vener-
able François, and I was sure he could de-
tect the clay from which a good servant
might be made. The making, if I took this
untried lad, would, however, be my task,
not his, and of my own powers in such a
direction I had the most profound distrust.
But just as my little "no," which is the
weakest-sounding word in my vocabulary,
was trying to make itself heard, François
took my cup of coffee from a footman,
placed it on the table, and left me with a
discreet air of having sown his seed, and
being ready to trustfully await its germina-
tion. And then the coffee did its work.
There is one short quarter of an hour in

every day I live—the quarter of an hour
after I know that I have had dinner enough,
and before I know that I have had too
much dinner, during which the summer
calm of contentment lets insidious currents
draw me towards what shoals they serve.
If a horse has ever turned out badly on my
hands, if a bit of money lent has not come
back to me again, if a small bet has proved
to be an altogether hopeless cast, the horse
has been bought, and the money lent, and
the bet made, during one of these quarters
of an hour. It poisons me, too, the coffee.
It's worse than the bread, and the red wine,
and the fourth cigar, and all the other for-
bidden fruits ; but for that little quarter of
an hour it lulls to sleep every doubt of
other men's clear rectitude and of my own
sagacity.

The excellent François knew all this, of
course. And he was not at all surprised
when I told him, half an hour later, that
the boy might come to see me in the morning.

It was raining when he came, and he
seemed to be a mere leaf blown from a

curb-stone tree. He was undersized and lean, and his eyes were too close together, and two monstrous ears sprang affrighted from his lanky fox-red hair. But he was very willing; that was all he had to say for himself. And he was ready to show that it was no idle boast. In the one moment during which he had stood before me his volition had fallen helpless before mine, like the fabulous bird at the gaze of the fabulous snake. His whole horizon was bounded by my wishes. His only estimate of what a fair beginner's wage would be was "as monsieur should wish." I don't think he used another phrase than that in all the course of our preliminary interview, except when he gave me to understand that his uncle had sent him to me with an intimation that if he failed to find favor in my eyes he need never hope for another recommendation. And then of course I was helpless. I told him that I would try him for a day or two, in order that we might see how we got on together, and that his first employment would be to help me move from the apartment I then occupied to the rooms I had taken in a hotel for the rest of the Paris season. I stood over him while he packed my boxes, or tried to make myself believe I did. As a matter of fact, I folded all my clothes, with a running commentary on the use and abuse of creases, and laid them one upon another with a disquisition on the art of packing trunks just full enough and not too full. When it was all done, and he had said " Oui, monsieur," some hundred times or more, he buckled all the straps, and then I thought the time had come to see what resources he had within himself. " I am going to breakfast now," said I, "and you must fetch an omnibus from the nearest railway station and move my luggage to the hotel, where the concierge will pay the driver, and where you may wait for me."

I met old Ledyard at Paillard's, and before we had finished our melon I had exposed myself to his unmeasured scorn.

" You are an owl, my dear fellow," said he—"an owl of the Apennines ; you will never see your things again. I am glad of it, for they are all abominable, and now perhaps you will let me choose some decent clothes for you, instead of leaping about looking like a fiend of the woods." I bore this abuse meekly, for Ledyard really is one of the best-dressed men in Europe, and his friends are all accustomed to his innocent belief that they look like either book-makers or dissenting preachers.

"Yes, my poor foolish friend," he continued, " this boy will lose all your atrocious trousers and all your obscene coats, and as soon as we have finished our steak we will go to your hotel, and we will have a fire, and you will give me some whiskey and Vals, and I will win all your money playing at écarté while you are fussing and fuming because your ragamuffin doesn't appear."

And, as it proved, he did win four games running before one of the hotel people came to the room to tell me that my servant and my luggage had arrived. The man said "the servant of monsieur " with a little look of astonishment, and when Hippolyte —for Hippolyte was his unhappy name— appeared, I forgave the impertinence. He had been by no means a smart-looking

youth when I first saw him in the morning.
His trousers were very much too short,
and clung so closely to his lean shanks
that they seemed to fade raggedly into the
drooping elastic sides of his rusty shoes.
His coat was as much too high in the neck
as his shirt-collar was too low, and its high-
waisted skirts were abbreviated in that
strange fashion which makes a Frenchman
of his class look like some absurd sort of
little bird. But now the effects were all
heightened. He was dripping with rain;
up to his knees the black liquid mud lay
as thick as if he had emerged from a bog
in the Landes, and from his knees up he
resembled one of those ingenious wall or-
naments of spatter-work which school-girls
used to make when I was a boy. But his
hat was in his hand, and he waited respectfully for permission to explain himself. I
asked him, carefully avoiding Ledyard's
eye, if the luggage was all there.

Yes, it was; and he regretted that he
could not have had it there two hours, or
perhaps even two hours and a half, earlier.
But there had been difficulties. It was rain-

ing so hard, and so many of the cabmen were
on strike, that all the omnibuses at the railway yard had been taken, and he had been
obliged to go to the central market and hire
one of the small hand-carts kept to be let
out to the hawkers of fruit, and then to
another *loueur* who kept tents to let for the
suburban fairs, in order to hire a tarpaulin
with which to cover the luggage. And on
the cart he had pushed his load all the way
through the wet streets.

Beaming beneath the rays of monsieur's
approbation, he went down-stairs to super-
intend the mounting of the boxes, and then
I had my little word back at Ledyard.

"You are no doubt in the right," said I,
"when you say that the only good servant
is a thoroughly trained English valet, and if
you only move from your place in the country to your house in London, he is never at
fault; but when you come to messing about
all over the Continent, and sometimes a farther shot than that, I am not so sure that
I'm an ass to prefer a man who doesn't
need to be handcuffed to an interpreter,
and who won't be forever telling me that

what I ask him to do isn't his work. A fellow like yours would have let those trunks crumble to dust before he would have dreamed of bringing them here himself."

"That's all very well," said Ledyard, "but chaps like that are too clever by half. You may think it's all very funny to pay sixteen guineas a dozen for your beastly *batiste* shirts, and then let a young monkey like that count them for the wash. But you'll be sorry yet that you ever saw his dirty face."

This I did not mind very much, for it is always Ledyard's way to be disagreeable when he has been winning at écarté, in order to disguise his pitiful exultation.

II

The next morning, when Hippolyte came to draw my curtains and prepare my bath, the contemptible pleasure which every one afflicted with moral cowardice finds in doing and saying amiable things lay smiling in my path. I told him that I thought he

had the making of a very good servant in
him ; and he repeated his little " Oui, monsieur," tacking to it the rider, " Soyez tranquille, monsieur "—a locution with which I
was afterwards to become painfully familiar.
But it was new to me as yet, and did not
jar upon my beatific sense of satisfaction
with myself and all the world.   Life is, indeed, a series of so trifling joys and sorrows
that even now I can recall to my face the
serene smile with which I awoke that morning.   I had sternly refused my after-dinner
cup of coffee the night before.   I had only
taken one glass of hock-and-seltzer in the
course of the evening, and I had left the
club with a few louis of my friends' losings
in my pocket.

"You cannot, of course," I continued,
"expect a very large wage at first ; I will
give you forty-five francs a month, and I
will furnish your clothing of every sort.
You will, indeed, be able, if you are thrifty,
to put by every sou of your earnings."   Hippolyte, with his stereotyped formula of assent and reassurance, gave me to understand that it would be his pride and his joy

to avail himself of so magnificent an opportunity to become a capitalist.

"You will," I continued, warming to my subject as I saw that it was a sunny day, and observed that the morning's post had brought me no tiresome letters to answer—"you will be lodged and nourished at my cost. The cost of your washing I will also defray. You will learn all that a gentleman's servant ought to learn, and I hope you will not be as ungrateful as most servants are."

Later in the day I put him by the driver's side on the box-seat of my coupé (an unpretentious but highly respectable vehicle supplied by a job-master), and drove off to an enormous emporium distinguished by the sign of the "Belle Jardinière." I had never before entered one of these gigantic outfitters' establishments, and it was not without a certain timidity that I alighted at its glittering portals.

Hippolyte, who had either been seeking enlightenment at the hands of the coachman, or had arrived by his unaided powers of reasoning at some theory of the functions of a servant on the box of a carriage, had leaped to the pavement with astounding agility, and stood with uncovered head awaiting my pleasure. He was still in his rags, and his bearing combined the dignity of a hungry dog with the elegance of a suburban footpad. At that moment I regarded neither Hippolyte nor myself with contentment, nor was I the better pleased when the affable person who received us in the vestibule of the "Belle Jardinière" gave me to understand that he supposed me to be a dutiful father in search of raiment for his son.

I never knew before how cheap clothing could be, or how expeditiously a man could attire himself, if he were not absurdly fastidious about the cut and fit of his garments. Hippolyte certainly was not. His coat and his waistcoat and his trousers and his overcoat and his mackintosh and his cravat and his gloves and his shirts and his collars and his wristbands and his underwear and his hosiery and his boots and his hat and his umbrella were, in his eyes, the most prodigious gifts that fortune could have brought

him. He would, I think, have preferred a
cravat of somewhat less sombre hue; and
an overcoat of a military cut profusely be-
frogged seemed to him more desirable than
that which I had selected. But he was
happy. He failed to see why he should
have garments especially designed to be
worn when he was in his bed, and explained
to me that it had always been his habit to
wear by night the linen that was no longer
immaculate enough to be worn by day. He
seemed to think, too, that I was unneces-
sarily lavish in the matter of toilet requi-
sites, but I told him that it was my wish
that he should have absolutely nothing at
the hotel except what I selected for him,
and that I expected him to take his morning bath as regularly as I took mine. It
was probably at the moment when I laid
this injunction upon him, and chose for him
a travelling-tub, that he arrived at the conclusion that I was a well-meaning person of
unsound mind. That this was his indul-
gent generalization I have been convinced
by certain of his subsequent methods and
achievements.

Ledyard, whose privilege it is to play the part of chorus to the simple drama of my life, heard all about it before the day was over. I knew that he would enjoy it, and I am afraid I take a shameful pleasure in baring my breast to his attacks.

"You will observe," he said to two or three of the Frenchmen who stood about the club fireplace patiently suffering his strange distortions of their language, "that our friend imagines he can make this lean and wretched lizard shiver in a bath-tub every morning. You are, my dear fellows, as a nation, the very dirtiest people in the world." Here Ledyard paused with the air of challenging the whole Gallic race to join issue with him. But no one answered; it only encourages Ledyard to contradict him. "You are, I say, dirty. I don't mean you fellows personally, because you and the other men in your position in life have learned from us Englishmen to wash yourselves." This generous qualification of his abuse, I am bound in justice to say, he expressly disclaimed when we were alone together. They were all filthy, every man Jack

of them, but he couldn't be uncivil about it.
It was, he said, an idiosyncrasy of his that
he never could bear to be uncivil to anybody, even Frenchmen.

"And when you come to the working-
classes, and people of that sort, they simply
cannot wash. It is not that they won't—
they cannot. When they are run over by
omnibuses and that sort of thing, and have
to go to the hospital, and the hospital people wash them, they die; that's all there is
of it; and that's what makes the death-rate
in a hospital so high. I was talking to one
of the biggest medical men in Paris the
other night, and I told him the same thing.
He said he had never thought of it before.
That's the way with all your doctors here:
they never use their common-sense. They're
altogether too scientific. As for this poor
devil of a boy, he'll have hydrophobia, that's
what he'll have; and he'll bite you, my buck,
and you'll go bounding up the Champs
Élysées with your horrid great tongue loll-
ing out of your mouth, and the gendarmes
will hack you to pieces with their little dull
swords."

2

Within a few weeks, however, Hippolyte
had learned, if not to take his bath every
morning, at least to put on a look of agreeable freshness with which to begin the day.
And he took so evident a pride in keeping
himself smart that I let him put away his
ready-made clothing from the " Belle Jardinière," and had some decent things made
for him by a tailor. The great Napoleon
is said to have begun to bully his friends
and antagonize his marshals from the moment that he first wore an imperial robe
bedizened with his short-lived golden bees.
And from the moment that Hippolyte perceived himself to have risen to the plane of
those who have their clothes adjusted to
their persons he entertained a fine scorn
for the unhappy wretches who are obliged
to adjust their persons to their clothes.
With me he was as mild as a May morning. His voice was low and pleasant, and
he taught himself a small deprecatory
cough, which he executed behind his hand
whenever he was overcome by his sense of
my surpassing splendor and his own un-
worth. But I heard him sometimes crying

in the waste places for hot water and for
towels and other matters, which it is the peculiar province of chamber-maids at inns to
forget and neglect. Then he was another
Hippolyte, and not a very nice Hippolyte.
His face was, indeed, the sort of face that
always looks as if it might, were it lifted
up, disclose a less civilized visage behind
it. His father—the working jeweller of the
Faubourg St. Denis—had come one morning to thank me for having taken Hippolyte
beneath my magnificent protection, and I
knew since then where the lad had found
his shifty eyes. I think that with another
look in them he used to glare wolf-like at
the poor stupid maids of the hotel. His
voice, I know, was the snarl of a beast of
prey when he pursued them to seek for
what I needed. I told him one day that he
would find a milder form of coercion equally effective, and much more conducive to
his personal popularity.

"Oui, monsieur. Soyez tranquille, mon-
sieur. Monsieur knows that they are all
Prussians, and more stupid than the pigs.
When monsieur does not like to be kept

waiting for his hot water—it is then that they are impossible, these Prussians."

One merit he certainly had, and that was that he was rigorously honest. I hate to have to lock things up, and as for making a practice of counting the small money in my clothes at night, I should go mad over it. There were always some *billets de banque* in my note-case, and more or less loose gold and silver in my pockets. And I thought it would be wise to make a little test to see whether anything stuck to Hippolyte's fingers when he emptied out my pockets in the morning before he took my clothes to brush. I tried him every now and then by making a laborious count at night, and solemnly noting down my total, and I always found when I made my comparisons next morning that every sou was there. When one stops to think what temptations such opportunities for petty thieving must present, one marvels that there are any honest servants in the world, and wonders, too, if it is altogether fair to them to try their probity so far.

III

The cold weather had come now, and I began to make my plans for the South. If I had carried them all out, these projects that I make at every year's end for three months' sojourn in the sunshine, I should have been able by now to write a guide-book to the south of Europe and the Orient. Sometimes I manage to get as far as Algiers, and once or twice I have accomplished a winter stay in Cairo, one of the most delightful places I know — to think about. It is always with a sense of virtue that I contemplate such flights as these. They are almost as heroic as a hunting winter in England. But somehow I always find myself at Monte Carlo before the end of January. I am ashamed of going there, and I make April vows each time that I will not go back again. Not that I lose money there, for I am a cold, half-hearted player, pleased to win a little, and never losing much, but because the atmosphere of the place reeks with vulgarity. I play games of

chance because the men I know best and
like best are always to be found where play
is going.   But the moment the play ceases
to be one of the lesser incidents of life it is
abominable.   One might as well keep a
shop and be done with it as always to be
counting money and *jetons*, and think of
nothing but gains and losses.

So I resolved to try Algiers again, and
put quite out of mind the thought that it
was, after all, only thirty-six hours across to
Marseilles and down to Monaco, if Musta-
pha proved too wet.   And as I was bent
upon taking a little run into the desert, I
thought it would be well for Hippolyte to
learn to sit a horse, in order that he might
go with me.   I asked him if he would like
to take riding-lessons, and he told me that
it had always been his heart's most cherished hope that he might some day find a
horse between his legs.   I made the necessary arrangement at the *manége* where I
stable my own hack ; and the senior riding-
master, who had often seen me trotting
around his *piste* when the mornings had
been too rainy for the Bois, assured me that

he would make a horseman of Hippolyte
in the shortest possible time. I was not
riding that month, for I am of a slightly
arthritic temperament, and I was at the
moment suffering from one of my occa-
sional touches of accidental gout—a mere
form of rheumatism, of course, but uncomfortable when one has one's feet in stir-
rup-irons.

Hippolyte was to take his lessons in the
early morning, and every day for a fortnight, when he came to wake me, I used to
ask him what progress he had made. And
every morning he used to tell me that he
felt a trifle stiff about the knees, but was
learning not to roll about much in the saddle. There even began to be perceptible,
after the first week, a horsy fashion in his
gait. And one day he came to my room in
breeches and leggings, apologizing for having been detained a little later than usual
at the *manége*.

"How many lessons have you had?" I
asked him. "You ought to have accomplished something by now, and it is only
necessary that you should be able to make

a journey in the saddle from time to time without falling off your horse."

Hippolyte went through a little panto-mime of counting his lessons on one hand and the Sundays he had missed upon the other, and announced that he had taken twelve in all, and that he thought he could ride well enough for practical purposes. So I told him that he need not go to the riding-school again. A day or two after, my foot was so much better that I told him to lay out my riding things. I noticed as he fastened the straps on my trousers that he seemed ill at ease, and I could not seem to teach him how to slip the spurs into their boxes. I asked him if he were ill, and told him that he must not sit up too late at night gossiping with the other servants, for lads of his age needed sleep. And then I drove up to the Rue Chalgrin to take my horse. While I was waiting for him to be saddled, I told the man behind the *guichet* to let me know how much I owed for the lessons, and asked if the riding-master was satisfied with the progress Hippolyte had made.

"The servant of monsieur has accom-

plished about as much as a beginner usually does," he replied, "but a gentleman so
profoundly versed in the art of equitation
as is monsieur knows that in only three or
four lessons but little can be done."

"Three or four lessons!" said I. "But
he's had a dozen, hasn't he?"

Just then the bell of the telephone behind his chair attracted his attention, and
he begged me to excuse him for a moment
while he answered the call. When he had
received the message he turned to me again
and said:

"I hope monsieur will not let the young
man know that I have said what I am about
to say, but the truth is that there have been
only four lessons, and that the young man
has this moment telephoned to me asking
that I should disguise from monsieur the
fact that there have not been twelve. I regret very much to be obliged to tell monsieur, but I do not see how I can well do
otherwise."

"Of course you couldn't, unless you were
going to rob me of the price of eight lessons, and leave me to discover in Algiers

that the young rogue doesn't know a horse's
head from his tail," I replied; for nothing
annoys me more than the sneaking way
Frenchmen of that class have of trying to
shield a servant who has misbehaved. And
then I rode down to the Porte Dauphine
and turned into the Allée des Poteaux, very
much out of humor at this absurd discovery.
But it's an old rule of mine never to chide
a servant while I am out of temper, and I
resolved to say nothing to Hippolyte until
the next morning. I think he hoped the
people at the riding-school had not betrayed
him, for, although his hands shook so that
he could hardly pull my boots off when I
came in from the Bois, he was as smiling
as ever when he dressed me for dinner that
night. I was dining at an English house
in the Avenue Kléber, and Ledyard was
there. At first I thought I would keep my
discomfiture to myself, but I cannot for the
life of me resist telling a story that seems
to me to be droll, even if it is against myself, and by the time fish was served I had
made a butt of myself.

"I know it's all very funny," I said to

Ledyard, as we drove away from the house, "but it's a nasty business all the same. I have had the young monkey for a couple of months now, and he's begun to learn my ways, and I've really taken a lot of trouble with him, not to speak of what his clothes and all that sort of thing have cost me. I've had him taught to press hats and how to take care of clothes, and I gave a man from my boot-maker's half a louis to spend the whole of one Sunday morning showing him how to do all kinds of boots. And now, after his making a fool of me in this fashion, he'll have no respect for me if I keep him, and he'll think he can play such pranks every day."

"It's a serious business," said Ledyard; "but in the meantime you might give me a light for my cigar."

"It is a serious business, whether you think so or not," I replied. Ledyard is the sort of man who imagines the winds of heaven ought to cease to blow when he has a cold in his head, but thinks nothing of another man's yacht having the sticks blown out of her; although I will say that he is a good fellow when you are ill. "It's a very serious business," I continued. "I don't know anything that makes more difference to a man than having a really good valet. The last fellow I had was a slow, hulking brute, and this boy is small and quiet and quick, and never under one's feet. It's all very well to talk about the important events in one's life, but it isn't being mentioned in General Orders or falling off your horse at a review that makes you happy or unhappy in the long-run. It's the smoothness of every-day existence, like having a good digestion, and if I have to break in a new man I sha'n't dare to look at a glass of Burgundy for a week."

"Of course the boy was an ass," said Ledyard. "It isn't one man in a hundred who would have been fool enough to take so much trouble over him, and you have certainly made a very smart servant of him in no time at all. But he was in a blue funk when he had to put his leg over a horse, and he lied about it, and thought he could pull wool over your eyes, as these beastly little Frenchmen always do. I don't

like his coming to your room in breeches
and gaiters when he hadn't been to ride.
That was what I should want to hide him
for. But I'd row him well if I were you, and
let it go at that. What do you want him
to ride for, after all ? · You're not going to Algiers, messing about among a lot of nasty
blackamoors. You're coming to Monte
Carlo, where I'll be, and where everybody
else that is fit to speak to will be. And
you want to look sharp about it, too. I'm
going in three days, and there won't be a
tom-cat in this hole a week from now."

And to Monte Carlo I went, taking Hippolyte with me, after rating him well. I
told him that he had been an ungrateful
scoundrel, and that he had tried to conspire
with the riding-school people to make me
pay them money for nothing, and that if he
went on in that fashion he would end up by
getting into the hands of the police, and
having his papers marked, and being ruined
for life. And then he wept copiously, and
declared that he had delighted in learning
to ride, and only missed his lessons because
he overslept himself in the morning, and

had hoped to make them up afterwards, and
all that sort of thing. And by the time we
were on board the Mediterranean Express
he was quite happy again, and trying to
atone for his faults by doing his work with
a dexterity and precision altogether remarkable.

IV

The sun shone brightly on the flowered
terraces of Monte Carlo the morning after
my arrival, but I had still preserved my
lofty tone, and I tried to make myself believe that I had only come in order to
take care of old Ledyard, who plays himself into a state of picturesque impecuni-
osity if there is not some one there to drag
him away from the tables when he has
made a winning.

"The whole thing," I said to him that
night at dinner, "is disgusting. Here's a
duke at the next table to us, a great leader
of public opinion and a man who has no
right to be in the same room with the worst
blackguards in Europe. And there at the

very next table is a scoundrel who has been kicked out of every club in London. And those people over in the corner ought to know better than to bring an eighteen-year-old girl into such a place. It's a good sound Warwickshire family. I know who they are. And the girl can't look up from her plate without seeing forty women that she must know are wrong. I'm not a strait-laced man, but I call it hideous, Ledyard."

"You've been losing," said Ledyard; "that's what's the matter with you. You're what I call chicken-hearted. When you lose, you lose; and when you win, you don't follow it up. And then you hate your dinner because the rooms haven't paid for it, and growl because you're not dining at Lambeth Palace. Why shouldn't the duke come here if he wants to? What's the use of being an English duke if you can't do what you please? I call it the finest position in the world, and that's just what makes it so fine. The royalties always have to be thinking what the radical newspapers will find to say about them; but a man like that can do anything in reason. There are

lots of men here I wouldn't play cards with ;
but then I don't have to.   And as for the
women, they wear smart gowns, and they
look pretty, and that's all I want to know
about 'em.   You're an old woman ; that's
what you are.   You're always thinking
about what you're afraid to eat, and what
you're afraid to drink, and now you're set-
ting up a moral indigestion as well."

"Monte Carlo wouldn't be worth coming
to if the people were all respectable," said
little Montgoublin, with whom we were dining.   "You say it's such a fine thing to be
one of your English dukes ; and they're
certainly better off than our people, most
of whom are too poor to come here at all.
But it would be no fun for them if everybody
in England were a duke.   It's just the same
way with the other thing.   There's no satisfaction in being an honest man if everybody else is as honest as you are.   We
three men wouldn't set ourselves up as an
example to the rising generation in the ordinary way, but we are in this place moral
dukes, there are so many others worse than
ourselves."

"I don't see it in that light," said I; "the place is a mire of iniquity, and it is only because we fellows have no personal substance that we don't flounder in over our heads and come to grief. A man who knows how to take care of himself, who knows his way about, as they say, is simply a cool-headed chap who has cooled his heart first. He keeps out of trouble just as a dry leaf blows over the surface of the bog. It's your hearty, full-blooded youngsters, who take everything seriously and themselves most seriously of all, who make fools of themselves."

"Not a bit of it," said Ledyard; "it's the dried-up old wretches like you who always come to the most dreadful grief. It's like hunting : you ride a young horse that knows nothing about his work, and he'll jump like a fool, and land in all sorts of places; but he'll scramble out again, because he's young and quick and has a good heart in him. An old screw like you, who's supposed to be safe because he's too weak to bolt and too sleepy to kick, will peck from sheer laziness, and once he's missed

3

his foot, over he goes without any effort
to recover himself. I'm not a great many
years younger than you, but I'm not afraid
of anything. Pretty woman that—just come
in the door. Who is she, Montgoublin?
She's never been here before. She looks
like an English woman."

"She isn't," replied Montgoublin, who
had already been at Monte Carlo for a
week; "she's a Viennese. Some women
speak to her, and some women don't. She
calls herself the Baronne Alixe de Sebenwald. But I think that's her maiden name.
Her husband was an Italian, and he used
to beat her, or she used to beat him, and
now he's dead or divorced or something.
Lady Dulverton had her over at Cannes the
other night, so of course she must be all
right. But the Italians make a nose at her.
If you want to know all about her, ask old
Tournielli; you're sure to see him over at
the rooms to-night, and he'll tell you in a
moment."

Before we had finished our cigars Tournielli himself, who had been dining on the
balcony, walked through the room, and Led-

yard beckoned to him. He took a seat at our table, and we asked him about the lady who was said to have beaten her husband.

Montgoublin had not apparently been very accurately informed. The late husband had not been an Italian, but an Englishman with an Italian twist to the end of his name, who had made his home in Venice. And there had been a story, of which the opening chapter had followed the prefatory nuptials without the customary interval of a blank page or two. The marriage, which had taken place in Italy, had been annulled by the Holy Father, and she had never spent more than two or three hours under her husband's roof. Her father had been an admiral in the Italian navy, and she had but a small fortune, with which she was at the present moment playing ducks and drakes at the tables. The elder lady who was with her in the restaurant was an aunt of hers, a sort of unsalaried companion and duenna.

"If you ask me," Tournielli replied, "whether the baronne is respectable, you leave me no alternative but to reply that

she is. I know her very slightly, but if it
would amuse you to meet her I think she
will permit me to present you. Speaking
for myself, I would not put my hand in the
fire for her. When a lady who is young and
good-looking has made a mess of her marriage, I don't think Monte Carlo is the place
for her. But she is received by some of the
best English people at Cannes, and they no
doubt know more about her than I do."

After we had finished our cigars we went
over to the rooms, and when I had lost the
modest ten or fifteen louis which I thought
a large enough straw to show that the wind
did not blow my way that night, I went to
the next *trente-et-quarante* table to console
myself by observing the misfortunes of my
friends. The baronne and Ledyard were
seated at the table side by side, and Tournielli, who was standing behind her chair,
had apparently made them acquainted, for
I could see that Ledyard was advising her
about her play. With the little flush of excitement in her cheeks, and the bright in-
tentness in her eyes, she was much prettier
than I had thought her when I saw her in

the restaurant. Her face had the peculiar
softness which is the characteristic beauty
of the Viennese, and she did not look more
than two or three and twenty. Her hair,
which was of the dull straw-color that one
sees oftener on a child's head than on a
woman's, lay in graceful-undulations—a disposition which never fails to please my eye,
and which is, I have been told, to be at-
tained by employing the services of a hair-
dresser at the cost of some twenty francs a
day. She had a little sheaf of five-hundred-
franc notes in her hand, and as I took my
place among the by-standers at the side of
the table opposite to her I saw her put two
of them on the red. She lost. Then she
staked four notes on the red again. This
time she won. And for a number of *coups*,
playing sometimes a smaller and sometimes
a larger stake, she continually added to her
little capital, which was enlarging itself like
a ball of soft snow rolling down a hill. I
was glad that she was not losing, but, on the
whole, I was sorry that I happened to be in
the rooms while she was playing.

I watched her snow-ball accumulate until

she had some forty thousand francs before
her, and then I saw her waver for a moment. Ledyard was evidently advising her
to leave the table. Tournielli, too, leaned
over and said a word in her ear. She had
been playing high, for a woman, and the
people at her end of the table all looked to
see what she was about to do. While she
hesitated, the croupier, who had glanced at
her, began to deal without any stake of hers
upon the table, and it resulted in what is
called a *refait*. The cards used for *trente et
quarante* are laid upon one line until their
pips aggregate thirty-one or more, and then
upon the other line. And the red line or
the black line wins as the total of one or
the other happens to least exceed thirty-one.
But both may hit upon this point of thirty-
one. This is called the *refait*, and when it
occurs all the stakes upon the table are, as
the phrase is, "put in prison," and must
remain where they were until the cards are
dealt again. If the color upon which you
had played loses this second deal, you lose
your stake ; and if it wins, you are not paid
any profit on your venture, but are only

permitted to withdraw your stake which had
been thus impounded. It is in this law of
the game that the advantage of the table
lies. Since there is an even chance that
you will lose upon the second deal, and
since you cannot win, the value of your
chance may be said to have been reduced
one-half by the occurrence of the *refait*.
And you are permitted, if you wish to do
so, to give the croupier half your stake and
withdraw the other half, instead of leaving
the whole impounded, and waiting for the
second deal. The *refait* occurs, it has been
computed, once in about every fourteen
deals. And yet each player hopes that he
will be able to make his little profit before
it has appeared. And, obviously enough, if
there were not some such recurring advantage for the table, the player, since he is at
liberty to increase or decrease his stakes all
the way from a *coup* of one louis to a *coup*
of six hundred louis, would be sure to win
eventually. He may, it is true, by paying
to the croupier an insurance of a few francs
upon every stake, purchase exemption from
the rigors of the *refait*. But the repeated

insurance premiums amount in themselves
to a considerable loss, and Madame de Sebenwald had not seen fit to pay this black-
mail to the robber *refait.*

And as the *refait* came while the baronne
was still trying to make up her mind what
she should stake, the customary sighs and
murmurs of vexation and astonishment rose
vaguely towards the frescoed ceiling, which
ought by now to be stained quite black
by all the angry exhalations it has known.
Some of the players said "*Partagez!*" to the
croupier, who thereupon confiscated half
their stakes, and gave them back the rest.
Others, greatly daring, trusted to the hazard
of the second deal, which resulted in favor
of the black; so that those who had played
the black, and had not compromised by
giving the croupier half their stake, recov-
ered the whole of it, but without receiving
any profit; while those who had staked
upon the red, and let their venture wait
upon the issue of the second deal, lost.   If
the baronne had played this *coup* in pursu-
ance of the policy she had followed, she
would have had her stake upon the red, and

the happy indecision which had stayed
her hand was one of those little favors of
fortune which superstitious gamesters especially admire. She had won seventeen or
eighteen hundred louis, a very tidy sum,
and after pushing her luck to the verge,
had refrained at the happy moment. I
wondered if she would begin again. She
rose from her seat, turned as if to leave the
table, and then paused. That moment of
doubt which comes to every player con-
tains the essence of a gambler's excitement.
Her hands, filled with the crisp blue bank-
notes, seemed to be drawn towards the
slow whirl of money on the table — that
eddy which twists away one's capital, and
at last, if one does not seize the occasion,
engulfs it. Ledyard spoke to her again, and
with a reluctant look at the cards in the
dealer's hands she left the table, and ac-
companied by Ledyard, Montgoublin, and
Tournielli, made her way through the spectators to a sofa in a corner of the room,
where they sat down together to discuss
the combat, from which she had borne
away the honors and the spoil. I was cu-

rious to see how she took her success, and
catching Tournielli's eye, I went over to
the corner, and was authorized by him to
make my bow to her.

"I am telling Mr. Ledyard," she said,
"that he was very kind to show me how to
play."

"I can't show you how to play," said
Ledyard. "Nobody can do that. All any
one can do to help you when you are playing is to try to keep you cool; but you
were not a bit upset, my dear child, and
you were in great luck to stop before that
dirty *refait* came."

"It was you who saved me," rejoined the
baronne, with a grateful upward glance at
his bald pate. And then Montgoublin and
I grinned at each other, while Ledyard
pulled out the swaggering ends of his great
gray mustaches. For we are always amused
when Ledyard adds another to the long list
of the women of all ages, nationalities, and
previous conditions of servitude, each of
whom he calls "my dear child," and each
of whom thinks he is the most charming
old gentleman in the world. There clings

to him, I think, some faint aroma of the day
when he was one of the greatest dogs in
all the Household Cavalry—a day in mem-
ory of which some sober dowagers still look
askance at him. He is even now as sol-
dierly, fine-looking a man as one could wish
to see, and with his hat on looks fifty at
the most. But why young ladies who are
young enough to be his daughters call him
" Bob," and wreathe his door - knob in the
Rue Marbeuf with flowers and pots of jam
when he is ill, I do not know. No such
engaging flatteries ever fall my way, and I
can only suppose that Ledyard's profound
belief that he is still a conquering hero
gives him the same charm that women find
in a precocious boy by whose innocuous
audacity they are amused.

.

V

The next day Ledyard took me to tea at
Alixe de Sebenwald's apartments in the
Villa Constance, and strutted about the
sunny room as if he had known her twenty

years. The talk soon turned upon play,
that inexhaustible subject of conversation
at Monte Carlo, and the baronne, who had
not been in the rooms that morning, and
whose winnings of the night before still re-
mained intact, again thanked Ledyard for
having shown her how to make a snow-
ball; for this simple process of letting her
winnings increase seemed to her a bottom-
less mine of wealth.

"If you take my advice," I said, "which
of course you won't, you will consider yourself uncommonly lucky to be a bit ahead
of the tables, and leave it at that. It's as
plain as possible that if you go on playing
long enough, and the cards run just as well
for you as they do for the tables, you will
lose every sou you have in the world. At
trente et quarante the *refait* makes a con-
stant advantage of about three per cent. for
the tables. At roulette there are thirty-six
numbers on the wheel, and the zero as well,
making in all thirty-six chances to one that
you will not hit upon the right number.
And if you do hit upon it, they only pay
you thirty-five times the amount of your

stake. So that in the series of thirty-seven
shots, if you hit it once, as you might fairly
expect to do, you would at the end of the
series have lost your stake once. On the.
whole, the percentage against the player is
larger at roulette than at *trente et quarante*,
and the men who play high, and play every
season, all play at *trente et quarante*. They
make a winning, once in a way, which seems
enormous if you forget how much they have
lost before they make it. But even the
three per cent. of the *trente-et-quarante* tables is hard to fight against. If they made
you play with counters instead of money,
and only sold you ninety-seven louis' worth
of counters for your hundred louis in money, you would think this discount was a
monstrous extortion; and when you remember that the shares of the company sell to-
day for five times what they originally cost,
notwithstanding the enormous expenses
which have to be paid out of the profits of
the rooms before a dividend is declared, you
can't help seeing that it is absurd to play."

"But it is very nice to win," said Madame de Sebenwald.

"Ask him why he plays if it's so hopeless," said Ledyard.

"I play because I am, like most of the nicest people I know, not so wise as I ought to be. But, on the other hand, I am not so foolish as many of them, because I do not play so high. I shouldn't care to be at Monte Carlo without playing at all. It's the custom of the place; it's in the air. Not to play at all would be like going about in a frock-coat and a top-hat. One plays because the others play, and if one did not play one would have a cold sense of being an intruder, like a one-legged man at a ball. I never lost more than three or four hundred louis in a season. When I begin to lose, I stop; and mine is only milk-and-water play at best. I never staked a maximum in my life."

" I have only been playing for a few days," said the baronne, "and as I am a winner so far, I think it's all delightful."

"You mustn't be too enthusiastic about it," said Ledyard, "because if you stick to it you'll drop a lot at it some day, and then you'll hate me, and I shall rush madly out

and hang myself to a tree on the terrace,
and dangle in the moonlight like the chaps
you read about in the newspaper."

"It seems to me the most interesting
thing I ever saw," said the baronne. "Of
course I've read a lot about Monte Carlo,
but when you read in a novel about how a
man staked so much and won it, and then
staked so much and lost it, it always seems
confusing and tiresome. But when you see
them play, and when you play yourself, it's
wonderful."

"It's cheaper to read about it," said
Ledyard. "But most of those fellows who
write about Monte Carlo come down here
for a week with a tourist's ticket, and live
at a little *pension* down Mentone way. They
play five-franc pieces at roulette, and they
don't know any of the men who really punt.
So far as playing goes, the only thing to do
is to let your winnings run, and cut short
your losses. When you do that you are
playing with the bank's money. I haven't
missed a season here for more than twenty
years, and I don't think there has been a
single day in them all when I haven't seen

a series of eight or nine blacks or reds in
succession, and counted up what I would
have won if I had started with a louis and
let it double up. It's a lovely set of figures.
I rattle them over in my sleep: two, four,
eight, sixteen, thirty-two, sixty-four, one
hundred and twenty-eight, two hundred and
fifty-six, five hundred and twelve, and then
if you win the tenth *coup* you've got a thousand and twenty-four louis, more than a
maximum, and have to take your money
off and go home. Only ten *coups*, think of
it! How I'd love to do it to-night! But
it takes an awful lot of pluck to leave it all
up. Fancy that tenth *coup*, when you've
already won over five hundred louis for the
one louis you started with, and you could
draw it off if you wanted to. You want to
howl with rage if you lose it, and yet if you
take it off, and then when the *coup* is played
you see that if you had left it on you would
have won again, you go and hammer your
head against the wall."

"I simply couldn't do it," said the baronne. "I should have to have my hands
tied behind me, or I couldn't leave it."

"I've done it two or three times in my life," said Ledyard; "thrown down a louis for luck, when I was standing up behind somebody, and not meaning to play at all, and then let it run into a maximum. And then how I swaggered out of the rooms and had a lot of people to dine! But I always say to a young man who asks me about play, 'Never touch a card—never!' I've said it a hundred times. I suppose I've lost, in all, forty or fifty thousand pounds playing here—for I used to play like a demon when I was a youngster—and there's nothing in it."

"I suppose it would be better for me not to play any more," said the baronne. "It's delightful to have won what I have, and I should feel dreadfully if I lost."

"You are quite right," said I; "but you will play nevertheless. Everybody makes good resolutions, and everybody goes back to the tables."

"Except," said Ledyard, "the man who won a heap of money and then built a big villa up on the hill, where he sits on his balcony all day and pulls faces at the Casi-

4

no, without ever going near it. But he was one man out of a million."

"And there are people," said I, "who believe that he is an employé of the administration, and that the whole performance was a put-up job to encourage people to believe that it is possible to beat the tables in the long-run."

"It is wonderful," said the baronne, "to think that there are ten millions of francs in the vaults of the Casino, and that the administration could draw on the bankers for as much more if they had to borrow money. Think what one could win in a single day if one only knew beforehand what the *coups* would be!"

"It is wonderful," said Ledyard. "And for that matter, I suppose there is hardly any limit to the amount of new capital they could raise if they needed it. But nobody ever has crippled them, and nobody ever will. All the stories you hear about men having broken the bank are the merest rubbish. It of course often happens that the amount of capital with which each table is equipped when the play begins may be ex-

hausted by a run in favor of the punters;
but as soon as the croupiers see that their
stock is running low, they send a man rush-
ing up-stairs to the office for more money.
And it has only happened once or twice
in the course of all the play I have seen
at Monte Carlo that a croupier has been
obliged to deal his cards or spin his wheel
a little more slowly to gain time until the
messenger brings him more money. The
administration of the Casino is one of the
strongest bodies in the world, and if people only knew more about the inside of its
affairs there would not be nearly so many
fools ready to lose their money. It is all
very well to say that the governments of
Europe ought to combine to put a stop to
the playing here, but if they could drive a
little common-sense into the heads of the
idiots who come here, that would serve the
purpose quite as well. To men like me it
really makes very little difference whether
they play or not. When we have a bad year
here—and the year is almost always bad—
we have to deprive ourselves of some of the
luxuries we like. But of course there are

silly boys—and silly men, too, for that matter—who cripple themselves for life in the
course of a single season. And yet, after
all, most of the play is harmless enough.
The men who play high are nearly all Englishmen, and Englishmen who are in the
habit of winning and losing large sums over
cards and horses at home. It isn't, after
all, the big fish who fill the nets of the Casino. The bulk of the money comes from
the people who lose four or five louis and
then stop. It is wrong, and it is immoral,
and it is everything you please, but still the
administration give you a good deal in exchange for your money if you don't play too
high. And as long as they do that, I don't
know that it's anybody's business how big a
profit they make out of it. It is the most
beautiful spot in the world, and it was nothing but a bare rock when they took hold of
it. Lots of people come here who hardly
play at all, and there are the orchestra and
the opera and the gardens, and all that, for
their benefit just the same."

"You know as well as I do, my dear fellow," said I, "that you can talk until you

are blue in the face, and you can't make yourself believe, let alone making anybody else believe, that this place isn't a sink of iniquity. It ought to be blown sky-high, the whole thing."

"I wonder," said Ledyard, "whether Madame de Sebenwald has ever heard the story of the man who threatened to blow it sky-high. They say it's true, but whether it is or not, it's ingenious. He was the commanding officer of a Russian man-of-war, this chap, and while his ship was at Nice he used to come over here every day and play like mad. He lost a lot of money, and then he began to help himself out of the ship's chest, like the bankers' clerks and such people, who think they can make good again. Finally he got to the end of the ship's money. He was a man of very good family and all that, and there was nothing for him to do but to write a letter to the navy people at Petersburg, calling himself bad names, and then blow out his brains. But he made up his mind he'd have some fun first, and he got up steam and ran down past Villefranche for drill.

When the ship was off Monte Carlo he went ashore in his launch, and marched up to the upper floor of the Casino, where he sent in his card to the chief of the administration. When he got into his office he said:

"'I have lost a lot of money at your beastly game, and I have robbed the ship's chest. I am going to kill myself, but first I am going to make it hot for you people. If you look out of the window you can see my ship lying off the port. My crew are not in the habit of asking questions before they obey orders, and I have had all the shore broadside shotted. I am going off there now, and I am going to blow your gingerbread building into so many pieces that the crows up on Turbie will be using thousand-franc notes to line their nests with. *Je vous salue, monsieur!*'

"And with that he started to walk out of the room. The man grabbed him by his braided coat-tails, and begged him to sit down and talk it over. The end of it was they gave him back all he had lost, and no one ever heard the story until he had retired from the navy."

"It would have been money in your pocket if he had blown it up, Ledyard," said I.

"I don't complain," replied that cheerful philosopher; "as long as I have enough left to pay my hotel bill when I want to leave I am satisfied, and the administration will always lend you your fare home. And now, my dear child, I must be going over to the rooms. It's the best time of the day to play, for all the little pigs that get the seats at the tables and scream with joy when they win tuppence three farthings have gone to their horrid dinners, and I'm going to win a million francs before I dress."

"She's rather an agreeable young person, isn't she?" remarked Ledyard, pulling up his shirt-collar and tucking in his chin, as we crossed the gardens on our way from the Villa Constance to the rooms.

"She seems to be an excellent listener," I replied. "I may be mistaken, but I don't seem to remember her having found a chance to do anything but say 'yes' or 'no' and gape at you."

"She ought to be uncommonly glad to have the chance, my funny little friend," said Ledyard. "My conversation is always agreeable and entertaining, whereas you sit flooding yourself with tea, and twiddling your thumbs over your poor old stomach like a rhinoceros on a music-stool."

VI

However much I disliked or thought I ought to dislike Monte Carlo, Hippolyte found it adorable. The hotel maintained a band of musicians to play for the ladies' maids, valets, footmen, and couriers while at table, and gave them champagne three times a week. He began, it seemed to me, in the sunshine of such joys, to blossom a trifle too luxuriantly. One morning he presented himself in an infamous cravat of white satin, bedecked with crimson dots and dashes, and I availed myself of the occasion to read him a little sermon. "You are," I said, "already provided with clothing appropriate to your condition in life,

"PRESENTED HIMSELF IN AN INFAMOUS CRAVAT
OF WHITE SATIN"

and when you spend your own money in
buying so monstrous a thing as that, you
do not succeed in making yourself look like
a gentleman instead of a servant, but like
one of the vulgar little shopkeepers you see
arrive here by the cheap trains every day,
persons whose position in life is one of much
less comfort and elegance than yours."

"Oui, monsieur; soyez tranquille, monsieur," replied Hippolyte. "Cela n'arriverait plus." Here was a new phrase which
was, I plainly saw, about to add itself to
the two flowers of speech to which I was
already used; and it seemed to me to mark
the appearance of a flaw in the clear crys-
tal of my treasure among servants. It had
the air of lying on the lower slope of a
moral declivity. The "Oui, monsieur" was
admirable. It was respect, assent, submis-
sion, everything that could be wished. And
then the "soyez tranquille" was a falling
away. It implied that there might be reason for me to need some reassurance. But
this new protestation, that what had oc-
curred should not recur, seemed to smack
of the sinner with whom amendment and

backsliding are a daily habit. It betokened an easy knack of self-condonation, unlike the abject remorse which had followed the incident of the riding-school.

"You may be sure, my boy," I continued, "that the greatest outward difference between gentlemen and people of the middle class lies in the fact that persons of that sort wear showy, tawdry clothes, and do not wash themselves. You have learned to take your bath every day, and you must try to believe that my taste in the matter of dress is better than your own. If you save your money, as I hope you will, and are enabled, after I am dead and have no further occasion for your services, to set up some little business for yourself, you will find that the experience you have had as a servant will have made you greatly superior, in appearance and in manners, to other tradespeople."

Hippolyte expressed his ardent wish that I might live to be a thousand, and permitted himself to observe that monsieur had a better mien in Monte Carlo than he had shown in Paris. But, like many other men

who are dreadfully frightened when they
are really ill, I find a melancholy pleasure,
when I am at my best, in contemplating
my approaching release from this unworthy
world's captivity. And I will say for Hippolyte that he was a servant to whom one
could talk, and that is a huge comfort.
With many servants you dare hardly ask
what the weather is, when you are called in
the morning, lest they take it upon themselves to chatter. But Hippolyte was the
most deferential of creatures, and yet had
none of that sense of personal abasement
which marks the manner of the free-born
Briton when he has to lace your boots.

When he had removed the offending cravat, I bade him run to the hotels which
Ledyard and Montgoublin respectively in-
habited, to ask them if they would not
drive over to Nice with me for breakfast.
They both accepted the invitation, and
when I had ordered the phaeton and pair,
which are held at my disposal by one of
the millionaires who enrich themselves in
the course of letting horses at Monte Carlo,
I wrote a little note to ask Madame de

Sebenwald if three dreary old gentlemen
could not prevail on her to make the day a
fête by going with them to Nice. And I
added that I hoped the cold of madame,
her aunt, was already better, and that it
would not be many days before that lady
would be well enough to go to drive herself. I was not very sure that the baronne
would go, but I did not see that she could
take grave offence at my asking her to go
without her aunt, notwithstanding that the
latter was no more indisposed than I. A
man of my age ought surely to have the run
of some of the minor audacities. And it
did not seem to me that a lady who kept
her duenna as severely in the background
as did this one hers, could find herself the
worse for driving to Nice with three old
fogies.

Apparently the baronne took my view
of the matter, for she sent word that she
would be ready at noon precisely, and did
not keep us waiting a moment at her door.
Her punctuality delighted me so much, for
I am never late myself and hate to be kept
waiting, that I started down the hill in the

highest good-humor, quite unruffled by the
stupid chaff of Ledyard, who asked, from
the rear seat which he occupied with Montgoublin, " Who taught you to drive — your
cornopean player ?"

The road which runs along the shore
from Monte Carlo to Nice is not, perhaps,
so picturesque as the lofty route of the Cor-
nice; but it is, none the less, one of the
prettiest drives in Europe. The stout little
horses which ply for hire all through the
Riviera season, and in the summer go to
climb the hills of the Savoy, make the run
in an hour; and it is one of the absurd
traditions of life in this little corner of the
world, where pleasure-seekers of all races
come to find their winter sunshine, that
those who stay at Nice shall drive to Monte
Carlo every day, and that those who live at
Monte Carlo shall go to Nice for luncheon.

Short as the road was, I learned a good
deal about my pretty companion before we
arrived at London House. And if the account she gave me of her position and her
purposes in life did not tend to raise her

greatly in my estimation, it at any rate suf-
ficed to awaken in my mind a curious interest in her proceedings. Ledyard and Montgoublin were busily forecasting the results
of an approaching pigeon-match, and, left
to amuse herself as best she could with me,
she passed the time by telling me much
more about herself than any well-bred Eng-
lishwoman would have cared to confide to
so casual an acquaintance — a garrulity
which I took to be one of the forms of that
strange want of the sense of privacy that
Englishmen observe in almost every sort of
foreigners. Her uncompleted marriage had,
it seemed, added nothing to her means,
and she had made serious inroads upon her
modest fortune by ill-advised investments,
and by the careless self-indulgence which
seemed to be a habit with her.

"It is a poor life I lead," she said. "My
home is in a stupid suburb of Vienna. I
have tried living in Florence, and I don't
think I like that much better. I can't afford
to live in Paris, and if I can win some more
money I think I shall make a trip around
the world. I don't suppose my aunt will

like it much; but I don't think she likes
anything. I am sure she doesn't like me.
But it is more fitting that I should have her
with me than that I should employ a stranger as my companion. I don't in the least
blame you for thinking she has a cold. We
shall have a very jolly time as it is, and she
would have been a nuisance. It is very
nice that you and Mr. Ledyard, who has
been so kind to me, are of a certain age,
because, if you were younger, I couldn't go
about with you. You see, mine is a difficult
position. A woman about whose marriage
there has been a story, even if she has been
as little married as I have been, is supposed
to go and live in a quiet place, and read aloud
to the rheumatic poor. I hate to read aloud,
and I detest the rheumatic poor. But I
lead a very prosy life of it, and what thanks
do I get? One or two of the English ladies
of whom every one stands in such awe are
gracious enough to receive me, but I suppose they would scold me for coming over
here with you. I am almost as entirely *dé-
classée* as if I didn't behave myself; but I
don't want not to behave myself: I want to

have plenty of money, and to amuse myself like other women of my own age."

"Why don't you marry?" I asked her. "You're young enough in all conscience—and pretty enough."

"Will you marry me?" she asked.

"That is no reply to what I said. I'm too old and too fond of my own way to marry anybody. But the world is full of young fellows with more money and more courage than I have."

"Of both of which," she said, "you no doubt think you would need an ample supply. But they don't want to marry me; I don't think they even fall in love with me. I have tried to make myself agreeable to one or two whom I thought *auraient pu faire mon affaire,* and they seemed to like me, in a way, but it didn't come to anything."

"Perhaps you show your good taste by liking yourself very much ; and I have observed that women who are what romantic people rudely enough call selfish, rarely arouse any strong interest in a man. One reads a lot about the magnificently cold-hearted women who make one man after another miserable for life; but when it comes to a man being fond enough of a woman to want to marry her, it is generally a woman of a more or less affectionate and disinterested disposition. She may change after she is married, and lead him an awful life of it, but she must have at any rate an outward softness to begin with."

"And you think I am hard?" she retorted, with a look out of her clear brown eyes that would have set Ledyard to talking any amount of nonsense. But I was busy avoiding a child that had been set out in the road to get itself run over, and earn *dommages-intérêts* for its parents, and I contented myself with saying that I thought her to be a very charming young woman with a highly-developed capacity for being good to herself in her own fashion.

She was silent for a moment, and then, as we crossed the Paillon, and turned the corner of the public gardens, she said: "I must wait until I find some old gentleman—not a clever old gentleman like you, who remembers wise things he has read in books,

5

and utterly confuses lone young women with
them, but an old, old gentleman who will be
pushed about in a wheeled chair, and buy
me all the sapphires in the Rue de France,
or else some one of your young English
milords fresh from the university, and so
shy that when I see him coming down the
street and give him my parasol to carry and
tell him to follow me, I can lead him into a
church and marry him before he has the
courage to say no."

"I think the 'old, old gentleman' would
serve the purpose better," said I, "and if
he were ever troublesome you could give
the wheeled chair a little push over the em-
bankment there, and let him run comfortably into the sea."

It was quite a merry breakfast-party.
People may talk about the " Paris " at
Monte Carlo, but I believe London House
to be the best restaurant in all the south of
Europe ; and the *maître d'hôtel*, who has all
the courteous dignity of the Russian grand-
dukes he delights to serve, is one of my
most cherished friends.   Perhaps the air of
Nice has something to do with it, for the

same people and the same plates and dishes
go to Aix-les-Bains each summer, and
there they poison you. Madame de Sebenwald was good enough to seem very much
pleased, and I own I like taking a smartly
dressed and pretty woman into a restaurant
much better than going in with only men.
It's like having a flower in one's coat—it
makes one look fresher and younger.

I knew Montgoublin to be fully as fussy
as myself at table, and I was amused to see
that the baronne listened with discerning
interest as I discussed the composition of
the menu with the *maître d'hôtel*. It is an
old saying among men of the world, and,
for all I know, may have been recorded by
some of the social philosophers, that a thoroughly good woman always shows the most
abysmal ignorance regarding what she eats
and drinks. And if, as she had said, Madame de Sebenwald's conjugal misadvent-
ure had tended to put her apart from other
women of her class in life, she had at any
rate the consolation of knowing a good
breakfast from a bad one. Although the
three Sacher restaurants in and about Vi--

enna are not, to my mind, so fine as their
patrons think them, a great number of discerning epicures are to be found among the
Viennese. The Hungarians, who spend so
much of their time in Vienna, are almost as
fond of good living as the Russians, and
hardly less profuse in their expenditure at
table. And they have imparted to the Viennese taste a certain amount of romanti-
cism, derived, no doubt, from the pictu-
resqueness of their own cuisine.

The baronne, I was glad to see, appreci-
ated the fresh caviar, which is, I think, to
be found in greater perfection at Nice than
anywhere else out of Russia. It was of the
delicate color of a hazel-nut, and each egg
large, firm, and well defined. She took but
half her glass of *vodki*, which I thought a
most judicious compromise between the timidity of the woman who eschews so excellent a digestive and the temerity of one who
tries to be as throat-hardened as a man.
She had enough regard for local color to
eat a little of her *nuna* salad, and when the
bortsch and *kacha* came, she poured the beet
juice on the clotted cream as eagerly as any

Russian. By the time we had finished our *côtelettes à la victime*, and modestly disposed of one magnum of champagne among the four of us, we were all in high good-humor, and Montgoublin and Ledyard, to whom she had confided her ambitious plan of travel, devoted themselves to an elaborate consideration of the precise *coups* by which she should achieve the preliminary conquest of the tables, and of the details of her itinerary. She took my pencil-case to draw upon the table-cloth a chart of her projected route, and Montgoublin told her that, for a lady who claimed the favor with which the fates are supposed to regard needy gamblers, she did herself uncommonly well in the matter of rings.

"I love my rings," she said; "they are my only barbarism; but, like all barbarians, I neglect my idols. I must give them to the jeweller in the *Galerie* to clean.

"You needn't do that," said I. "His charges are based upon the prodigality of winners, and I'll send my servant to you, who used to be a jeweller by trade, and will clean them for you quite as well."

"Or elope with them," said Ledyard, "and then we'll all have to melt up our watch-chains and have them hammered into new rings for you."

"If I were you," said Montgoublin, " I should spend at least six months in Japan, and bring away a Japanese house which you can put up at Monte Carlo, and the most beautiful kimonos in the world, and then you shall have us all to dine, and we will sit cross-legged on the floor."

" Bring a jinrikisha, too," said I, "and you can put Ledyard in the shafts, and make him pull you up and down the hills."

"You shall put me anywhere you wish, my dear child," said Ledyard, " and I will do anything you bid me. These men lead gluttonous lives, but I am a simple creature, and have kept my heart young. It's eating that ages people, always. And I consider myself very lucky in having made so light a luncheon, for we shall certainly be upset on the way home, and I will seize you delicate-ly in my arms, and bound gracefully into a place of safety."

But no such calamity disturbed our return

journey, and we all went to the rooms for
an hour before dinner, where Ledyard lost
furiously, and the rest of us did very little
by way of either gain or loss.

.

VII

I sent Hippolyte to the Villa Constance
next morning to clean Madame de Sebenwald's rings, as I had told her that I would do.
And he was evidently very much impressed
by the daintiness of her little belongings.
He came back to me quite flushed with enthusiasm. The *femme de chambre* of madame
la baronne had been very much pleased to
be taught the little trick of cleaning the
repoussé toilet battery of madame, and
madame had never known before that
mounted brilliants should be boiled from
time to time. And madame la baronne had
been *gentille*—" Ah, pour çà, on peut bien
dire qu'elle est gentille !"

It further appeared that the Obliged
Lady had offered the Pattern of Servants
(all Hippolyte's impressions took an Orien-

tal cast) a present of a Piece of Gold, the
which had been Respectfully Refused,
upon the ground that the Mighty Potentate,
whose Slave and Thing the Boiler of Diamonds was, had wished to make the
Rose of Beauty a gift and present of the
services of his Admirable Artificer. And
then there had been discovered, under the
trays of a jewel-case (where all manner of
worthless rubbish seems to hide itself), a
useless morsel of Venetian chain, attached
to an absurd old goggling eye-glass, and
this Hippolyte had permitted madame la
baronne to force upon him as a token of
her approbation of his necromantic stew-
ings and fryings. And he trusted that
monsieur would understand that he could
not have well declined a recompense so
purely honorific. All this was very well for
me to learn, but when Hippolyte attempted
to dilate upon the incredible number of little jewelled flagons which stood upon the
lady's toilet-table, and upon the unsurpass-
ing beauty of her *chevelure*, as she sat drying
in the morning sun, it became necessary to
repress him. I suppose the poor lad had

never seen a lady in so intimate a guise before. The simple decency and comfort of my own appurtenances and manner of life had been to him, when he first came to me, a marvel of magnificence. And the delicate confusion and warm perfume of a woman's room, at such a time of day, must indeed have been a revelation to his untutored senses.

At about eleven, when all the world of Monte Carlo suns itself upon the terrace, pleasingly entertained by the screams and roars of the trains which pass beneath, and the re-echoing gun-shots on the pigeon-ground, I found Madame de Sebenwald in search of Ledyard.

"I thought I should be sure to find him here," she said, "and he is always so kind and nice that I wanted him to do something for me. I entered my little toy terrier Goliath for the dog show at the Condamine, and he was there all day yesterday. I don't see why I should have to leave him there again to-day and to-morrow. The judges looked at all the dogs yesterday. There are only sixty-nine entries, you see, and they have announced that there will be seventy-five prizes. I entered poor Goliath because I thought that he would be so pleased and proud if he could get a prize, and I suppose he will have the prize now whether he stays or not. You see, they charge you half a louis when you enter your dog, and a louis for the cost of the medal when he gets a prize, so by giving all the dogs prizes, and a few of the dogs two prizes each, everybody is pleased, and they make a very good thing out of it. So, I fancy, they won't make me leave him there to-day if I tell them he is tired. But Mr. Ledyard is so clever, and they all have such a respect for him, whether they understand what he says or not, that I thought I would ask him to walk down there with me. It's a pleasant stroll from here, and when one is coming up the hill again one can talk tremendously fast, and try to be too much interested to notice that it is a climb."

"My French," I replied, "is not perhaps quite so remarkably constructed and so ornately decorated as his, and I am afraid I lack his splendid fierceness of manner.

But I incline to believe that even without his assistance we can persuade those grim functionaries to let you keep the terrier at home, without losing the privilege of paying them a louis for a silver five-franc piece with the name of your dog engraved upon it. My own experience has been that Englishmen can't get anything out of Frenchmen by bullying them. As soon as you rub their fur the wrong way they become so excited, and they so jabber and sputter, that you can't reason with them. It is for that reason that the police all over France have to be so arbitrary and so rough. If they let a man whom they are about to arrest try to explain that he is innocent, he makes such a noise about it that he breeds a riot."

"The French are very tiresome in a great many ways," said the baronne. "I am sure that I should like English life much better."

"English society," said I, "is very like a little green oasis with a lot of hot, disgusting sand on every side. If you once get under the trees you have an uncommonly jolly time of it, but as your chief occupation and amusement is trying to keep other people from getting in, there are a good many left out on the bare sands, and that isn't so funny. I know an old fellow who belongs to three or four of the best clubs in London, and who makes no bones about saying that he blackballs every man who is put up for any of them. ' I'm in,' he says, ' and the harder it is for the other chaps to get in, the more satisfaction I take out of being in myself.' And I fancy that a good part of the British pride and exclusiveness that people talk so much about rests upon the same foundation."

"English people are pleasant enough when they are here," said Madame de Sebenwald.

"Yes," said I, "because they have left their doctors and parsons and officious friends behind them, and are eating what they please every night, and doing what they please Sunday morning, and giving their morals a general holiday. So, of course, they are good-natured. We should all be good-natured, all the year round, if we didn't have to take care of ourselves,

and try to do our duty in the station of life
to which we have been called, and the rest
of it. Everybody is more or less a slave,
one way or another. I knew a man once
who devoted a number of years to a laborious attempt to completely eradicate from
his nature all sense of right and wrong, and
all sense of shame. He spent the five fort-
unes of his five sisters, for whom he was
trustee, and railed against Heaven for not
having blessed him with a sixth sister; he
was caught cheating at cards, and seemed
rather delighted than otherwise when people
wouldn't speak to him. Take it all around,
he enjoyed about as absolute a liberty as
any man can, and still keep out of the hands
of the police. And then, when he had saved
up his ill-gotten gains, he began collecting
Louis XVI. clocks, and became such a slave
to the habit that he barks like a dog when
the Cluny collection is mentioned in his presence, and rolls on the floor when he thinks
of the clocks at South Kensington. It's a
queer world."

"This is a very bright corner of it, at any
rate," said the baronne.

"That it is," said I. "The days slip by one after another, and there is every day some new story about the tables, and every day pretty women and smart gowns one hasn't seen before. And the best of it all is that you go to bed early, and it's one of the very few places in the world where you do that. A month from now, or two months from now, you and I will probably be where we are now, and you will have won a little on a lucky Tuesday, and lost it on a cruel Wednesday, and won it back again, and lost it back again, and we shall none of us be much the richer, or much the poorer, or much the better, or much the worse in any way."

Prophecy is but a poor exercise of the imagination when matters of play are at issue, for the next twenty-four hours were to witness one of the most remarkable exhibitions of gamblers' folly in my experience at Monte Carlo. I strolled into the rooms the next day after breakfast, and saw Madame de Sebenwald sitting at one of the *trente-et-quarante* tables, playing maximums. She lost three *coups* running, a total of

thirty-six thousand francs, obstinately back-
ing her belief that a run upon one color
was not likely to continue. And this is
beyond any doubt the maddest form the
gambling fever ever takes. The third *coup*
I saw her lose left her with only one five-
hundred-franc note before her, and this she
put upon the red, and lost again. It was
all infinitely silly; and it is my belief,
grounded upon some knowledge of the
course of life at Monte Carlo, that any
young and pretty woman who plays high
risks more than her money, and is apt to
forget more sorts of prudence than the
mere sense of caution about louis's and
francs. I liked the baronne, if I didn't approve of her, and I was sorry to see her
launched upon so dangerous a tide. But
to give her her due, she had rare pluck for a
woman. Her mind had, of course, suffered
that strange loss of balance which a succession of heavy losses seems almost inva-
riably to produce, but outwardly she was as
cool as you please. I have seen a notorious
English money - lender, who is said to be
one of the few men the administration real-

ly fears, lose four and five hundred thousand francs at a sitting, and rise from the table without a twitch of his knowing old face. And the baronne was, to all appearances, as unmoved as this giant among players could have been. As I approached her with some purpose of tardy remonstrance and useless consolation, she said: "Le voilà parti! All my winnings are gone," and she smiled as prettily as if she had only mislaid a glove.

"At any rate," said I, "don't be foolish enough to come back to-day."

"That is certainly good advice," she said, and left the rooms.

I saw Ledyard at another table, and went to see what he was doing. He hit a little run upon the red, then lost it all, and with only a few louis's in his pocket went over to the roulette, the last resort of every player out of luck. After fiddling about for a few *coups*, he put three louis's on the thirty-two, *en plein*, and won. This good-luck flushed him, as good-fortune always does, and for the next few *coups* he had gold pieces all over the last half-dozen. In a half-hour he

had, after making several tidy winnings,
lost it all again; and we went back to the
trente-et-quarante room where the baronne
had been, half fearing that we should find
she had been to the bankers to draw money, and returned to fight against a bad
day. And there she was. She must have
come to Monte Carlo with the determination
sooner or later to risk all she had, in the
hope of making a winning that would not
only supply her with the funds necessary
to make her voyage around the world, but
leave her with a little income afterwards.
Ignorant, apparently, of the familiar truth
that it is fatal to attack the tables with too
large a capital, she had at least two hundred bank-notes of a thousand francs in
front of her, and it was evident from the
close attention of the croupiers, and the
presence of a knot of spectators about her
chair, that a battle royal was in progress.

"Go and tell her not to be such a fool,"
I said to Ledyard. "From the way she
talked to me the other day, I don't believe
she has much more than that in the world."

"I'll try," said Ledyard, "but it's no
6

use; I've been there myself. She'll only
swear, when it's all over, that my speaking
to her cut her luck."

"Never mind," said I, "you can stand
it. Somebody ought to speak to her, and
you know her better than I do."

I followed Ledyard as he elbowed his way
to her chair, and heard her, in reply to his
whispered expostulations, say, in a hard,
strained voice : "Je vous prie, monsieur, ne
me dérangez pas."

"There !" said Ledyard, when we got out
of the crowd again ; "I knew I'd be jolly
well snubbed for my pains."

"It makes me sick," said I, "to see her
making such an idiot of herself. It's all
very well for a man ; if he is an ass, nobody
suffers for it, unless he has a family. And
a man can always do something for a living
if he comes a cropper. But it's awful for
a woman who has no one to look after her
to lose her money that way. It sickens me.
Let's walk over to Cap Martin. It 'll do
us both good, and if we stay here she'll
swear we flurried her."

I went to my hotel to get a stick, and

then Ledyard and I followed the white,
sunny road to the pleasant grove of pines,
and asked Tournielli's wife to give us a cup
of tea. It was very pleasant to get away
from the stir and glare of life at Monte
Carlo for an hour, and to see the little Tour-
niellis teasing their puppies and ponies.
The happy, boisterous mirth of children always warms my heart when I know that I
shall not see them again for a month or two.

VIII

When Ledyard and I returned from our
long walk to Cap Martin, we went into
Ciro's to drink a whiskey-and-soda, and
there we found Montgoublin, who told us
that the baronne had indeed come to grief.

"She was simply mad about it," he said,
"and she hardly won a single *coup*. When
it was all over she walked out of the rooms
looking so white that I went up-stairs and
told the head man he had better send one
of his people to the Villa Constance to tell
her maid to keep an eye on her. She looked

like doing herself a mischief, if ever anybody did."

I thought, and Ledyard with me, that we ought to go and leave a card upon her, although, no doubt, she would not want to see us. It isn't easy to know just what to do in such a case. People who have come to grief don't want to be troubled by officious friends, and yet it seems heartless not to make some show of interest.

We were neither of us sorry when her maid told us that she was lying down and had left orders not to be disturbed, for I don't think either of us would have known just what to say if we had seen her.

I was dining at a house upon the upper hill that night, where there was whist after dinner. But I met Montgoublin again on my way back to the hotel, and he told me he had heard no news from the Villa Constance. So it seemed pretty clear that if Madame de Sebenwald had made any desperate resolution she had at any rate not attempted to carry it out that night. People who like to know everything that is going on are sure, at Monte Carlo, that if they have heard no news there has been no news to hear; for all the world is so continually rubbing shoulders in the little place that every tale worth carrying is told within an hour.

"It's been a big day all around," said Montgoublin, "wonderfully high play for so early in the season. There was a young fellow, a Neapolitan, some one said, who came into the rooms just after dinner and put down a louis on the black. I didn't see it, but the fellows who were there say that he didn't seem to have ever played before. It seems that he let his louis run for a series of ten blacks, and then complained because the croupiers wouldn't let him leave on more than a maximum. At any rate he seemed to think that what they wanted him to do was to move his money over to the red, and he hit five maximums there, and after losing one switched back to the black. The end of it all was that he got a hundred and fifty thousand francs, they say. I suppose it's one of those beastly little Jews."

"I wish it had been the baronne instead,"

said I, and went home to my hotel with
rather a heavy heart. I hate to see people
I know get into trouble. I fancy it's partly
because I know they generally ask one to
help them out again, and partly because
they are not good company when they are
in the blues. How much of a more humane
leaven there may be in my regret I don't
pretend to say, but at any rate such disas-
ters always make me dismal.

The day's surprises were not over yet.
I found a note for me at the hotel from
Ledyard, enclosing a few lines from the
baronne to him.

"*J'ose guère m'adresser à vous, cher Monsieur,*"
her note ran, "*mais je suis au désespoir. J'ai fol-
lement perdu tout ce que je possédais au monde—
jusqu'au dernier sou. Il ne me reste que de m'en
aller à Vienne chez des parents, qui m'aideraient,
sans doute, d'une façon ou d'une autre, mais tou-
jours d'assez mauvaise grâce. D'abord il y a ma
semaine à payer à la villa, et puis il y a les frais du
voyage. Pourriez-vous me prêter deux cent louis?
Si je ne trouve pas l'argent autrement, je vendrai
mes bijoux à Vienne plutôt qu'ici, ce qui me ferait
subir une grande perte, et des désagréments que vous
comprendrez bien.* ALIXE DE SEBENWALD.*"

Ledyard had passed on this appeal to
me : " I'm awfully sorry for the poor child,"
he wrote. " But she might as well ask me
for two hundred moons as for two hundred
louis's. I have only about eighty in the
world to pull me through till quarter-day.
If you are ass enough to want to help her
out, you might tell her that I had intimated
to you that she was in some temporary want
of funds after her bad day."

It was altogether very disagreeable. If
she had written to me instead of Ledyard,
I didn't see how I could have very well said
no ; and I felt the more kindly disposed
towards her that she had not done so. For,
after all, she knew him but little better than
she knew me, and, if she could make up
her mind to ask either of us, I thought I
was very lucky that she had not pitched on
me. It seemed to be going a little out of
my way to offer to lend her the money. If
I wanted to be very chivalrous about it
I could give Ledyard the four thousand
francs, and let him lend it to her, without
her knowing that any one else knew she
had asked him for it. But after all, a

hundred and sixty pounds is a good deal of money. According to her own story, as I remembered it, her people in Vienna were not very near relations, and if they didn't help her, and she had to sell her jewelry and go out as a governess, I might or might not get my money back. So far as fifty pounds went, I thought I would be willing to stand that, but at a place like Monte Carlo, where everybody you know is always getting into a hole, a man has to learn not to be too kind-hearted. My general rule is that any man I'll bow to I'll lend ten pounds to. I'm not a poor man, any more than I'm a rich man. I have what people call a decent income. But I know plenty of things that cost a hundred and sixty pounds that I would like to have, and that I do without. Altogether, I thought I would let the letters lie till morning, and sleep over it. If she hadn't killed herself already I didn't think she would get up in the night to do it, and her note to Ledyard did not impress me as having been written by a woman who was likely to proceed to extremities. And I was making myself

ready for bed, when Hippolyte came into
the room. I never made him sit up for me
at night, because I think that if you expect
your man to be up early in the morning, so
as to do your boots and all that sort of
thing before you ring for your bath, you
ought to let him get to bed in good time.
So I was rather surprised to see him, and
not too well pleased to see that he looked
flushed and excited. It was a pretty business, I thought, if he was going to begin
drinking just as I had him well broken in.
I asked him rather sharply what he wanted.

"I have come," he said, "to say to monsieur that I have been in the *salle de jeu*
this evening."

"You did very wrong, then," said I.
"You know that it's against the rules for
servants to go there, and you had no business to go to such a place, whether there
was any rule or not. I wonder they let
you in."

"Monsieur will imagine," said Hippolyte,
"that when I asked for my admission-card
I did not say that I was a servant."

"Then you must have told them a lie,

for they always make a man state his position in life when he applies for a card.   I
suppose you have lost all your savings, and
it serves you quite right.   If you go on
playing such tricks I shall discharge you
one of these fine mornings, and then you'll
wish you had put something by to fall back
upon.   Now don't bother me any more, for
I want to go to bed."

"I beg monsieur's pardon," rejoined Hippolyte, with a quiet little air of satisfaction,
"but if monsieur should see fit to give me
my *congé*, even to-night, I should have something to fall back upon.   I have a hundred
and thirty - four thousand five hundred and
sixty francs, fifty centimes."

"A hundred and thirty - four thousand
fiddlesticks !" I exclaimed. "You've been
drinking, Hippolyte, that's what you've been
doing."

"Monsieur will permit me to say that I
never drink anything except at the table,
and then wine cut with water," replied Hippolyte, "and I have this moment counted
the money."

And without any air of braggadocio he

produced from his pockets an enormous
roll of notes and a handful of loose gold.

I was fairly staggered at this, and then
I remembered Montgoublin's story of the
man who had made a big winning just before the rooms closed, and saw that the
supposed Neapolitan must have been Hippolyte.

"Very well," said I, "you ought not to
have gone to the rooms ; but as you did go,
I suppose I should be glad you had such
good-luck. Of course you don't want to
continue to be a servant, when you have as
much money as that, and if you take my
advice you'll ask the hotel people to put it
in the safe for you to-night, and swear on
the crucifix never to gamble for a sou again
as long as you live."

"Oui, monsieur. Soyez tranquille, monsieur. Cela n'arriverait plus," said Hippolyte, with his accustomed docility. "But
monsieur will need me until he has had
time to find some one else. And if monsieur could not find a servant here, I would
stay with monsieur till he returns to Paris."

I thought this very decent of the lad, and

told him so, and then I sent him away, and composed myself to sleep. But all these extravagant adventures had upset my nerves a little, and, although I wished Hippolyte well, and was glad that he should have a chance to better himself in life, I was nevertheless a good deal more put out at the prospect of having to teach a new man my ways than at Alixe de Sebenwald's misfortunes. Hippolyte had been, after all, very well off as he was, and would probably put his money into a shop and lose it all; whereas, if she had struck his luck instead of hers, she would have been happy and smiling, as I like a pretty woman to be.

I read more than half of a tedious French novel before I could sleep, and in the morning it was an hour or two later than my wonted time before I rang for Hippolyte. He had put my drawing-room in order, and brought in my boots and clothes as usual. His quiet, neat way of moving about a room seemed very pleasant, as I thought how soon I was about to lose him. And I really felt quite an affection for him as I asked him what the weather was.

"Monsieur will find it a little cooler than yesterday, but quite fine," he replied. "And here is a letter for monsieur."

While he went to fetch the water for my bath, I opened the note, and fairly began to think that all the world had gone mad. It was from the baronne, and was as follows :

"MY DEAR FRIEND,—I cannot write your English, but you will see that I am so touched by your goodness that the French is too cold. You are so generous at me I can say nothing. You send me your relief without a word, and I have no words. I will not rest at Monte Carlo. I will take the train before the play begins to-day, that I will be sure not to be again foolish, and will let my aunt and my maid come later carrying the trunks. *Dieu vous bénisse! J'ai le cœur plein de votre bonté.*

"ALIXE DE SEBENWALD."

"Ledyard," thought I, "must have found the two hundred louis's for her somewhere else, and she got some muddling idea in her head that it had come from me. I suppose he told her he didn't have the money himself, and she thought I had let him have it for her. I must write and tell her she is wrong, but I'm not sorry she's clear away." With this sage reflection I betook myself to my tub, and after I had disposed of my tea and toast I walked around to Ledyard's rooms. He was already out, and I found him on the terrace.

"What on earth is Madame de Sebenwald writing to thank me for?" I asked him, showing him her letter. "I got your note last night, enclosing hers, but I waited until morning to make up my mind what I had better do about it, and now I get this from her."

"I'm sure I don't know," replied Ledyard. "I haven't done anything about it. You might go to the Villa Constance and ask her aunt."

"Madame the aunt was engaged in making her preparations for departure," the baronne's maid informed me, and I told the woman that I had received a note from madame la baronne concerning which I wished to communicate with her at once, as, although its envelope had been addressed to me, it was evidently intended for some one else.

" I will take to Vienna any letter monsieur desires to send to madame la baronne, but as for the note which monsieur received this morning, I took it to the hotel myself; and it was in reply to a letter monsieur's servant had left for madame a few moments before."

I left the villa growling to myself at the stupidity of the woman, who had evidently mistaken some one else's servant for mine, and met old Tournielli. He greeted me with a quizzical look on his face and said:

" You couldn't give me a few million francs this morning, could you?"

" I believe you're as mad as all the rest of them," said I. " What are you talking about?"

" It is only that the Baronne Alixe, whom I have just put on the train, tells me you are playing Monte Cristo to everybody, and I might as well have my share of the treasures of the island."

" My dear Tournielli," said I, taking his arm and drawing him over into the garden, " will you be good enough to tell me precisely what you mean?"

"I mean," said he, "if I must be so categorical, that Madame de Sebenwald told me, not half an hour ago, that you had been so moved by her ill-fortune that you sent her more than half the amount she lost yesterday, and sent it enclosed in a huge envelope without a word. And I mean also to say that I am not quite sure whether you are a very much richer man than I had supposed, or whether my little friend Alixe has quite turned your head."

"Tournielli," said I, very seriously, "you will be good enough to accept my explicit assurance that I have never, either directly or indirectly, given or lent to Madame de Sebenwald one single sou, that she has never asked me for a sou, and that you, or she, or both of you, are under some extraordinary delusion. And you will also, I hope, be good enough to never repeat one word of this farrago of nonsense to any one. You and I are old friends, and you can see that a story which, if it were true, would place both the lady and myself in a position of some delicacy in the eyes of the world,

is the more offensive to me when it is without foundation."

I left him there, staring bewildered at a
cactus, and went to my rooms, where I
found Hippolyte counting my things for the
wash. As I walked into the room, he said:

"If monsieur will retain me in his service I should be grateful. I have lost the
money."

"Lost the money!" I exclaimed. "The
rooms were closed when I saw you last
night, and they haven't opened yet to-
day."

"I have lost it," said Hippolyte. And
then repeated, quietly: "Oui, je l'ai tout
perdu."

And that was the last word which ever
passed between us on the subject.

IX

After the departure of Madame de Sebenwald, life at Monte Carlo resumed its wonted course, and, although the season had on
the whole been a very pleasant one, I was

7

not sorry when the warmer weather of the
early part of April called me back to Paris.
I think those of us who lead a migratory
life are almost as glad to return to the
North in the spring as we are to leave it in
the autumn. The smiling face of the Riviera sky becomes a hard-set grin, and one
longs for the familiar sights and familiar
faces of Paris, of which one had been so
consummately weary only a few months before.

And more than all I was glad to get back
to my clubs, to see once more the great
easy - chairs, and to hear the gossip of the
men who know all the latest *potins* the day
before they reach the ears of the world at
large. My hack had wintered excellently,
and the leafy alleys of the Bois seemed
very delightful after the hot sun of Monte
Carlo.

Of the baronne I had heard nothing
more. I had written, in as few words as
possible, to tell her that the money had
not come from me, and let the matter rest
at that. To the repeated questions of Ledyard and Montgoublin I had simply replied

that I had not lent her a sou, and that it did not seem to me to lie within our purview to make any conjectures as to the source of the deliverance she had found. I had said to myself at Monte Carlo, when Ledyard had asked me to assist her, that if I liked her I did not at any rate approve of her, and now I began to doubt whether I had even liked her. At all events she had now passed out of the narrow limits within which my simple life is spent, and I make and lose too many pleasant acquaintances every year to be seriously concerned about those who have betaken themselves to other fields.

It was in this agreeable condition of entire satisfaction with myself and my environment that I passed the first few weeks after my return from Monte Carlo; and then it became necessary to decide whether I was going out of town for the first of May. There were disquieting rumors in the air. It is the agreeable habit of the working-men of Paris to celebrate "Labor Day" by not doing any labor at all, and by making themselves as unpleasant as they

possibly can. Sometimes there is dynamite; and dynamite is not a pretty thing.
And, apart from the possibility that when
you cross the Boulevard on the way to
your May - Day breakfast you may find
yourself between a mob of rioters on the
one side and a squadron of the Garde Républicaine on the other, there is another
excellent reason for passing the day out
of town. When the streets of Paris are
not watered, the whole city is enveloped in
a cloud of dust. And when the municipal
authorities anticipate trouble they leave
the streets unwatered, partly because cavalry can work to better advantage when the
asphalt is not slippery, and partly because
the choking dust tends to drive the disor-
derly classes into the wine - shops, where
their enthusiasm expends itself in drinking
beer instead of in breaking windows. It
lessens, too, the throng of mere spectators
who on all such occasions greatly hamper
the police in their endeavors to control the
enemies of public order. And it is, plainly
enough, a prudent man's business to keep
out of the streets at such a time.

But when Ledyard and I discussed the
matter the night before Labor Day, we arrived at the conclusion that there was nowhere out of town to go. One of the clubs
to which we both belonged had a long balcony on the floor above the level of the
street overlooking the Place de l'Opéra, and
we finally decided that we would breakfast
at this club and pass away the afternoon in
watching from this point of safety the dem-
onstrations of the malcontent.

All the newspapers that morning were
filled with more or less alarming prophe-
cies, and all recounted, to the last detail,
the precautions which the ministry had tried
to take as secretly as possible. There were,
according to these accounts, large bodies
of troops posted in ambush everywhere
about the quarter. The court-yards of all
the public buildings had been occupied by
soldiery the night before, and at the first
alarm the Boulevard and the neighboring
streets would be completely cleared.

At about two o'clock, when we had finished breakfast and taken our places on
the balcony, the Place was thronged with

poorly dressed people, of whom lads not over twenty years of age seemed to form the greater number. They seemed well enough disposed, but the police had some trouble to keep them moving, and shrill cries of "Circulez!" arose on every side. There was no attempt on the part of the mob to mass its numbers in any sort of order; but there was an evident, and apparently a preconcerted, disposition to impede, rather than to resist, the efforts of the police to prevent a stoppage of street traffic. Arrests were frequent. If a man did not move on when the police told him to do so he was immediately marched off between two gendarmes. And the captures thus made became every moment more numerous. There seemed to be no anger and no violence on either side. The police did their work sharply and brusquely, but without, so far as we could see, anything that could be called brutality. Nor were there, as yet, any attempts on the part of the mob to rescue the prisoners captured. Now and then the crowd would obstruct the passage of the police towards the post where they were conducting their prisoners, but even this attempt to embarrass them in the performance of their functions seemed to be more by way of horse-play than by way of serious disorder. One man would push another in front of the gendarmes so as to block their way for a moment, rather than get in their path himself. On the whole, it began to seem as if the day would pass without any great trouble.

But when we had been upon the balcony about an hour, there began to be a perceptible change in the attitude of both the police and the mob. Each arrest made entailed a dozen others, for the prisoners began to cry to their friends for assistance, and the latter would push about the police until it became necessary to arrest them in turn. The throng, too, kept pouring in through all the channels which converge at this central point of the city, and it became clear that the Garde Républicaine would have to be employed. This body of cavalry, which performs in the streets and parks of Paris the functions of mounted police rather than of soldiery, has a very summary fashion of

riding over mobs. And at its first charge
the broad open space was cleared alike of
gendarmes and of rioters, all of whom fled
helter-skelter from under the horses' hoofs.
For perhaps twenty minutes the Place was
quiet, and then the gendarmes proved un-
equal to the task of holding the streams of
men pent in the streets, and for a moment
the Place de l'Opéra was again a sea of
struggling people. Then there came another charge of the Garde, and then another
interval of quiet.

"That is all there is of it, now," I said
to Ledyard. "These fellows don't mean
fighting. We may as well go in and play a
chouette."

"I don't see it," said Ledyard. "Every
few minutes there'll be a noise in the
streets, and then every man Jack at the
table will be jumping up from his chair and
flying madly through the window, and there'll
be such a beastly confusion that no one
will know whether a king has been marked
or not."

"As you like," said I; "but I don't want
to stay here all night."

" I don't suppose you do," said Ledyard,
"but you had better dine here, and then
go home quietly in the evening. At nine
or ten o'clock these idiots will have had
enough of it, and the streets will be clear."

"That's all very well," said I, "but I
want to dress before dinner. I'm all over
dust and filth here, and I'm going to look
in at a reception in the Avenue Kléber after
dinner, so I must dress."

"Then you had better send a man for
your things," said Ledyard, "and dress
here. You don't want to be pushed about
among these dirty wretches; and if you're
going to do it, you had better do it now,
for it may be worse towards dinner-time,
and then he won't be able to get through."

I thought this was a good suggestion, and
I sent one of the club *commissionnaires* to
my apartment to tell Hippolyte to bring
over my dressing-bag with the things I
needed. The man had to wait at the door
nearly half an hour before he could cross
to the Boulevard des Capucines, and then
we watched to see how Hippolyte would
succeed in crossing when he came. I knew

that when the gendarmes saw him carrying
a bag they would help him make his way
through the crowd, and I knew, too, that he
was not the sort of lad to get into trouble. While we were watching for him a cab
appeared from the direction of the Gare
du Nord, laden with luggage, and stood
blocked at the mouth of the Boulevard
des Italiens, unable to cross the Place.
Ledyard, whose eyes are very keen, said :

"Do you see the initials on those
trunks ?"

I could not make them out myself, and
he said :

"The things are marked 'A. de S.' I
wonder if it's our friend the Baronne
Alixe ?"

As he spoke a lady put her head out of
the cab window and called to the driver to
try to make his way across the Place. It
was Alixe de Sebenwald.

At this moment a man standing at the
corner of the Rue de la Paix got into a
scuffle with a gendarme who was trying to
arrest him, and the free fight which resulted
called down another charge of the cavalry.

When they had cleared the Place, a policeman told the driver of the baronne's cab to cross while he could. But the horse, frightened by the tumult, reared and balked.

Just then Hippolyte appeared at the corner of the Boulevard des Capucines with my bag in his hand, and, seeing that it was a favorable opportunity, made a run for it to get to the club door.

Suddenly a man in the front rank of the crowd stooped, and, with a long sweep of his arm, such as one uses in the delivery at bowls, sent a round black kettle whirling through the air towards a group of some hundred gendarmes who stood massed together near the cab. I heard the cry, "It's a bomb!" Hippolyte heard it too, and, dropping my bag, stared at the black object as it rolled towards the gendarmes. It caromed against the curb of one of the little refuges in the middle of the Place, and, its course deflected like that of a billiard-ball which has touched a cushion, rolled towards the cab instead of towards the gendarmes. It struck the rim of one of the wheels and stopped.

I could see the fuse smoking.

The baronne saw it, too, and cried: "*Mon Dieu, la dynamite!*"

And then I saw Hippolyte run towards the cab. He stooped, and I could see him fumbling with the bomb. The driver had leaped from his seat, and he and all the gendarmes were running for their lives.

A man beside me on the balcony, quicker witted than I, cried to Hippolyte: "Pull out the fuse!" And I heard Hippolyte, not twenty yards away from us, answer: "*C'est trop tard!*" The fuse had burned so nearly to the iron that he could not get hold of it.

He picked up the bomb, and, holding it in his two hands, poised at his shoulder, started to run as if to gather impetus to fling it farther from him. While he was still holding it, and when he was about a rod from the cab, his foot slipped on the pavement, and he fell full length upon the bomb, lying like a football player on a ball.

And then the explosion came.

I ran from the balcony to the stairway, and as I pushed my way to where I had

seen him fall, I said to a rough-looking
fellow who was in my path : " Let me pass.
He is my servant !"

The man stared at me a moment and
said :

" No, *bourgeois*, he is no one's servant
now."

It was true. I had lost Hippolyte, there
in Paris where I had found him. And all
so recently that it is almost an indelicacy
to talk about him.

GOLDEN-BEAK

.

LLOYD OSBOURNE

VAILIMA IN SAMOA

Give this, my dear Osbourne, to your mother for me. As the old saw has it: "Gratefulness is the poor man's payment."

G. B.

Paris, 1894.

GOLDEN-BEAK

LYING back in my long cane-chair, as the steamer swept broadly round the corner of the absurd city of San Francisco and awoke to the slow swing of the sea, I was very glad to have left America behind me. I knew that I was in the wrong; I knew I ought to have stayed in the United States long enough to live down that first aversion which almost every Englishman who visits the country finds awaiting his arrival, like a letter from home, and of which he possesses himself with a sturdy British satisfaction. But I was on my way to Japan, where I had been before, and was glad to go again, and the journey from New York to California had been a prolonged discomfort. The dust

and the heat had repeated themselves in the
faces of my fellow - passengers, and now I
had left all the nastiness behind me, and
promised myself three weeks of summer
air and summer calm.　I had not been well
when I left England, and the fatigue and
annoyance of the long railway journey must
have put a line or two more in my face.
For as the ship slipped past the headlands
(which are beautiful, and be hanged to
them!) I saw some one standing over me,
and a pleasant, childish voice said :

"Won't you let me give you one of these
cushions ?　You look so ill."

I looked up, and saw a fair - skinned,
yellow - haired little woman regarding me
with as much of friendly interest as if she
had known me for years.　She spoke with
a strong American accent, and I was very
tired of that manner of speech.　Her speaking to a stranger was in itself audacious,
and of the quick audacities of American
usage I was more than weary.　But she was
pretty, and there was clear kindliness in her
eyes.　I took the cushion, telling her that
she was very good, but that I was in fact

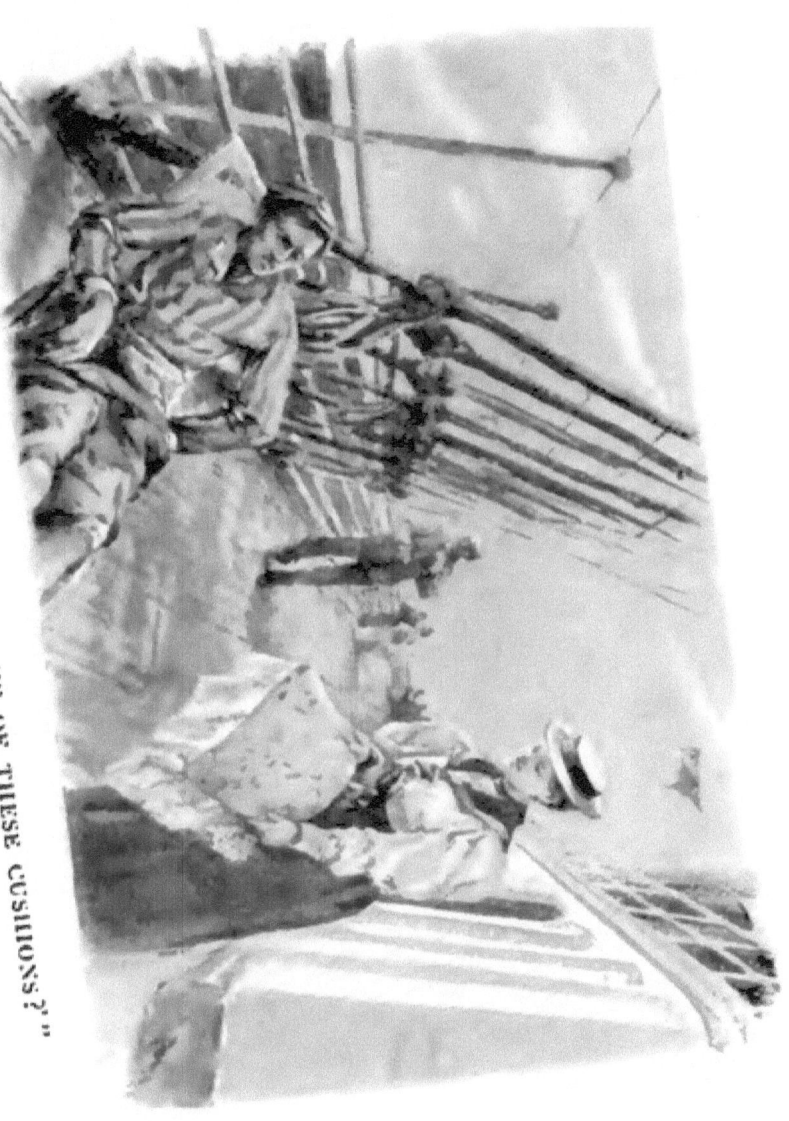

"... WON'T YOU LET ME GIVE YOU ONE OF THESE CUSHIONS?"

more tired than ill; and as I put it behind
my head I observed that it was strongly
perfumed with *eau de Chypre*, an odor I pe-
culiarly dislike. Still, I was glad to have
something between my head and the chair-
back, and I fell asleep with the convic-
tion that women were, after all, good-heart-
ed creatures. When I opened my eyes, an
hour later, the deck - steward was running
about, laden with particolored rugs, and I
told him to send the head-steward to me.
When that functionary appeared I made the
little speech which I always made to steamer
stewards, and which I can confidently com-
mend to travellers who like to be comfortable at sea.

"Here," said I, "are two sovereigns for
you. If I find that I am better cared for
than the other passengers, you shall have
two more at Yokohama. And here is my
card, which you will give to the purser, telling him that I should be glad to have a seat
at his table."

"Yes, sir — thank you, sir," said the
steward; "and is there any one on board
you would like to sit by at table?"

"No," said I; "I don't know anybody here—but you might give me a seat next to that lady with the blue rug," and I indicated the owner of the cushion.

"Mrs. Potwin, sir," said the steward. "I will speak to the purser, sir." Whereupon I went to sleep again, wondering where any one had unearthed so hideous a name as Potwin.

When my servant came to tell me that it was time to dress for dinner, I asked myself, as I changed my blue jacket for a black one, whether I had done well to demand a seat near the lady of the yellow hair. In all probability she had a husband with her, and while one may forgive a pretty woman the name of Potwin, as one excuses the monstrous appellation of an orchid, a man with such a name must necessarily be atrocious. But when I took my place at the table she sat at the purser's right hand and I at hers, and I saw that Potwin must be among the missing or the dead. The purser, although in some ways not a bad sort of fellow, had the affability of his calling quaintly combined with the

uneasy pride of station which seems to dis-
tinguish all Americans who are not day-
laborers. His name, he told me, was Chamberlain, and he gave me to understand that
the family of Chamberlain occupied about
the same position in the United States as
the house of Howard in England. There
is, no doubt, a certain inconvenience latent
in the absence of titular distinctions in
America. A man has to be always telling
you that he is a duke. This particular cadet
of the family of Chamberlain had, he pro-
ceeded to tell me (with one of those bursts
of confidence in which American aristocrats
delight), dissipated his patrimony before he
left college, and, too proud to toil for a live-
lihood under the shadow of his ancestral
palace in Fifth Avenue, put his broken fort-
unes to the hazard of the sea. When he
had thus conclusively demonstrated that he
was no every-day sort of ship's purser, he
presented me to Mrs. Potwin, and I thanked
her for her kindness in the matter of the
cushion.

"Oh, you needn't be so grateful," she
said ; and when she smiled she was certain-

ly very pretty. "It made me feel lonesome to see that we were actually off, and I was glad to have an excuse to speak to somebody."

I sent for some champagne, in compliance with the inscrutable rule that a passenger who is distinguished by the purser's consideration shall always keep that gentleman's glass filled, and, after dinner, Mr. Chamberlain asked me to come into his cabin and smoke my cigar. When I saw how liberally the steamship company had provided for his comfort, I perceived that the purser of an American boat in the China trade was a personage of no little importance. The room in which he slept was twice as large as that for which I had been made to pay a huge sum of money, and the office in which he received me, and in which he never seemed to have any work to do, was as big as the ship's smoking-room.

I was very sleepy, but I can vaguely remember learning that he had more white shirts and more suits of white linen clothing than the captain himself, that the owners winked at his doing a little quiet trading on his own account, that he was an honored guest in the English clubs of Yokohama and Hong-Kong, and that I had shown great knowledge of the fitness of things in sending my card to him, and asking to be placed at his table. The captain was, I further learned, a most ignorant and unmannerly individual, only to be commended for his good sense in recognizing that he had not nearly so great a "pull" with the steamship company as had the purser. I am not sure whether it was on that occasion or later in the voyage that Mr. Chamberlain explained to me that the owners had become his slaves and things because he knew all about their evasions of the law restricting Chinese immigration; but I know, at any rate, that he talked to me for a long time, and always of himself, and that I was exceedingly glad when it was time for me to go to my own less magnificent cabin and sleep the sleep of the bored.

When I went on deck next morning I found that the deck-steward had placed my chair beside that of Mrs. Potwin, and if I

was somewhat inclined to resent the train
of reasoning from which he had inferred
that this disposition would meet my views,
I was not sorry to be amused by her chatter. I knew, as soon as I had seated myself in my chair, that I should hear her
whole history, and I knew, too, that the
opening chapter would be a dissertation on
the profound rootage of her family tree. I
knew also, since she was young and pretty
and travelling alone, that the second chapter would concern itself with an unhappy
marriage. There are, no doubt, young and
pretty married women who travel alone on
their way to rejoin husbands they adore,
but in the course of much going to and fro
over the surface of the earth it has never
been my fortune to meet one of them. All
those I have known have been abused an-
gels, and most of them victims of the
world's unjust censure as well as of marital
brutality.

I had the pleasure of patting my fore-
sight on the back. It was ten o'clock when
I came on deck, and by noon, when the
purser came to invite Mrs. Potwin and my-

self to partake of a very rare and precious
sort of cocktail which he was about to com-
pound, I had the story. As for the gene-
alogy, it proved, as is often the case with
American genealogies, to be rather a record
of the political and financial achievements
of the uncles and cousins of the narrator
than a tale of past ages. They were all
rich and great, it appeared, the men, and
the women all unhappy and frequently con-
soled. Mrs. Potwin's father had, like many
other rich and great men, sought less simple
joys than those afforded by his hearth and
home, and the mother of Mrs. Potwin had
run away with a gentleman who wore gold
lace on the sleeve of his coat. The brilliant
creature whose effulgence had cast this dark
shadow over Mrs. Potwin's childhood was
not very clearly described. At one stage of
the narrative I conceived him to have been
military attaché at one of the embassies in
Washington, and at another his portrait
seemed rather to be that of an *écuyer* in a
travelling circus. At any rate, the mother
had run away with him, and my young
friend had found herself " standing with re-

luctant feet " bereft of maternal support.
It is a general law that young and pretty
women who are travelling alone have never
known a mother's love, and perhaps it is because they have all lost their mothers early in
life that their husbands have been permitted
so truculently to ill-use them.   Potwin had
appeared, and she had promptly disliked
him, and as promptly married him.   It was
a long story, but, accent or no accent, she
had a soft little voice.   At this hour I cannot be sure whether she married Potwin
because she had a step-mother, and was
unhappy with her, or because she thought
she might some time have a step-mother and
be unhappy with her.   That Potwin was a
monster I need not say.   We have all been
taught in school that if we want to get a
clear idea of any character in history we
ought to try to imagine him present to our
gaze, and to my sight Potwin appeared with
a keg of rum in one hand, a cudgel for his
shrinking bride in the other, and tender
words, addressed to an obese lady, upon
his sinful lips.   Whether Mrs. Potwin had
divorced him because he beat her, or he

"A VERY RARE AND PRECIOUS SORT OF COCKTAIL."

had divorced her because he was tired of
beating her, I was not quite clear; but they
two were twain.   I ventured to ask her if it
was because she liked the sound of Potwin
that she had abstained from resuming her
maiden name, and she told me it was out of
regard for the feelings of her family.   Upon
this we went to the purser's gilded office,
where he poured five different fluids together and stirred them up with a broom.

   In the course of a week we had become
very friendly, the little Mrs. Potwin and I.
Whatever her shortcomings, or long-goings,
may have been, she was a young woman of
uncommonly quick perception, and it did
not take her long to discover that I was by
no means inclined to make a fool of myself for the sake of her pretty yellow hair
and her soft blue eyes.   She told me that
she believed Englishmen to be singularly
lacking in the imaginative faculty, and I
was rather pleased than otherwise that she
should excuse my want of enterprise as a
racial defect.   I liked to hear her talk about
herself, but I had no desire to have her
set other people talking about me.   I was

charmed to fill her wine-glass, as well as the
purser's, but I did not want to have her
discover when we reached Yokohama that
there had been a mistake about her letter
of credit, and to have her ask me to lend
her a hundred pounds. The young ladies
who have never known a mother's love, and
whose husbands have behaved like brutes,
have a little habit of being unbusinesslike
about their letters of credit. In a word,
Mrs. Potwin was a delightful acquaintance,
but did not impress me as a person with
whom I cared to cultivate an enduring
friendship; and as for losing my heart to
her, I should as soon have lost it to a fairy
in a Christmas pantomime. My generaliza-
tions were, as I afterwards discovered, more
or less unjust. She was not an adventuress.
She had a very comfortable income of her
own. She wanted somebody to talk to, and
accident threw me in her way. She could
not help dropping her eye-lashes at me:
that was second nature to her, and she was
frankly disappointed because I would not
fall in love with her. She believed that she
was a woman made to disturb the souls of

men, and she resented my placidity. Three
or four young fellows among our fellow-pas-
sengers were quite mad about her, and even
the purser himself (who gave me to understand that he not infrequently found favor
in ladies' eyes, he remaining untouched of
heart) followed her about like a large and
proud sort of dog before we reached Honolulu. The steamer was to lie there all one
day, and Mrs. Potwin told me it was her
pleasure that I should take her for a drive;
so we went together to the Pali. I was
flattered by her preference, for I knew that
the young fellows had one after another in-
vited her to go, but before the drive was
over she explained the compliment away.

"You see," she said, "they are all in love
with me, or anyhow most of them, and the
rest will be before we get to Yokohama.
They all look at me as if I were a plate of
ice-cream, and I like that — I like it better
than anything else in the world; and they
quarrel about me all the time, and that is
perfectly lovely. But if I went off and
drove with one of them you wouldn't be
miserable at all—you wouldn't care a bit.

I don't blame you for it: it is because you are an Englishman, and you can't help it; but they are not as stupid as you are, and they appreciate me. There'll be awful rows before we get to Yokohama; you'll see. One of them walked to the stern with me last night, and while we stood looking over at the phosphorus he was holding my hand so I wouldn't fall overboard, and you know it was as calm as calm. I suppose you are horrified at that."

"No," said I, "I don't know that I am horrified, but I don't think it is a very pretty thing to do. It is quite possible that when you have let the young man hold your hand he goes back to the smoking-room and tells the other youngsters about it. It would certainly be wrong if he did, but young ladies who flirt with casual young men do expose themselves to that sort of thing."

Then I saw Mrs. Potwin in a new phase: Mrs. Potwin in a temper. She jumped out of the carriage (fortunately we were toiling up a hill), and vowed she would go back to Honolulu on foot; that she would never speak to me again; that no one had ever

spoken so rudely to her before; that I was
not a gentleman; that no Englishman ever
was a gentleman, and much more to the
same effect. And of course I had to beg
her pardon seven times before I was for-
given. If I had lost my heart to the whim-
sical little woman I might have thought all
this very charming, but as I had not, it
seemed very absurd and indecorous for me
to be coaxing her back to the carriage within
eyesight and earshot of the English-speak-
ing Kanaka driver, while she was stamping
her little shoe-heels into the mud and calling the whole island to witness that I was
no gentleman.

I was sorry too, when the time came, that
we had arranged to dine together at the hotel that evening, for after a brief visit to the
ship she came ashore again, dressed as if
to go to a ball, and was delighted to find
that every man in the dining-room stared
at her all through dinner. And then and
there I determined that when we reached
Yokohama, where there were civilized English people who knew me, and whom I did
not want to have talk about me, I would

not gild my person with the splendor of Mrs. Potwin's rays. This was, no doubt, a wise resolution to make, but when I made it I did not know that Mrs. Potwin's given name was Ysonde, nor did I know that, instead of being only a flippant, flirting little person, Mrs. Potwin was a lady whose purpose in life was to occupy a throne.

II

It was not until we had crossed the meridian of one hundred and eighty degrees that I began to be seriously interested in the career of Ysonde Potwin. On the evening of the day when we had first begun to count ourselves east of Greenwich instead of west of Greenwich, I was listening to the purser's stories with a patience born of long practice, when I amazed myself with the discovery that he had something new to say.

"Have you noticed," he asked me, "that there is anything strange about our friend Mrs. Potwin?"

"I can't say that I have," I replied. "She

is an American, you see, and I have not
known a great many American women ; and
I don't think we have women of precisely
her sort in England. With us they are either
a little more careful or a little less careful."

"I don't mean that," said Mr. Chamberlain. "She is a dreadful little flirt, and of
course she is divorced, and there are all
sorts of stories about her. But haven't you
seen anything remarkable in the way the
Japanese take care of her ?"

"No, nothing very special," said I. "They
are very quick and attentive, as Japanese
stewards always are, and I fancy that servants, like other people, are always ready
to wait on a pretty woman."

"There's more than that," said the purser.
"I have to keep my eyes peeled on board
this ship, I can tell you, and there isn't
much going on that I don't know. You
see, I really have most of the responsibil-
ity. The engineer tells the stokers to keep
the boilers hot, and that's all he has to do.
The captain tells the quartermasters to steer
the course that the chart shows, and that's
all *he* has to do. And between them they

9

keep the boat moving until the time comes
to drop anchor. But whether she is moving or not, my work goes on all the same.
Here are all of you passengers, cooped up
on board like animals in a menagerie, and
I have to see that you are fed and kept in
order. You see, I have two difficult classes
to deal with—the drunkards and the missionaries. When we touch at Honolulu there is
always a lot of men going down there to have
a spree. It is a regular Fiddlers' Green for
the men who keep respectable eleven months
out of the year, and then make even with an
awful racket. They come from as far east
as Chicago, just to go down to Honolulu
and let off steam a long way from home.
Then there are all the wild young fellows
whose families send them off to Japan and
China because they have been getting into
trouble. And when there is too much whiskey-and-soda in the smoking-room, or when
the poker game gets stiff enough to make
mischief, I have to remonstrate. Sometimes
it's ticklish business. The pursers on the
boats from New York to Liverpool are nothing but baggage-masters. Any fool could

do their work. But on these long runs a man has a great deal to think about, I can tell you."

I expressed my profound respect for the moral sway exercised by Mr. Chamberlain, who continued :

" As for the missionaries going to China or coming home again, they are always quarrelling among themselves, and their wives always pick on some woman aboard the ship and say she ought to be put down in the steerage because she wears better clothes than they do. And the worst are the missionaries' wives on the way home from China. They have got in the habit of being waited on by a lot of cheap servants out there, where the converts wash dishes for the sake of being under Christian influences. And when they get on board they have to look after themselves and their babies, and they won't turn out of their cabins in the mornings, and altogether they lead the chief steward a dreadful life. So you see I have to keep a kind of general supervision over everybody's morals and manners. And there is something very queer about Mrs.

Potwin. I don't mean that she doesn't behave herself—she's a lady as far as I know, and I make it a rule to take people as I find 'em—but the steward's Japanese boys are all afraid of her. He knows Japanese ways and Japanese tricks as well as most foreigners, but he says he can't make it out. You know there is always one steward they call the captain's boy, who stands behind his chair at table and looks after his cabin, and it is always an understood thing, in the pantry aboard a ship, that the server takes care what he gives that boy to take to the skipper. The first thing that the chief steward saw was that the captain's boy was changing plates, after he left the pantry, with the boy that waits on our end of my table, and that Mrs. Potwin was getting the bits put by for the captain. I never heard of such a thing in my life. I have seen young fellows with loads of money—what we call 'high-rollers' in California—chuck the boys five-dollar gold pieces as if they were quarters, but no one ever saw anybody else get the captain's portion of a turkey before. What do you make of that?"

"If you say it is unusual I have no doubt it is," said I, "but it isn't a very grave matter, after all. I hardly think the captain is likely to starve to death."

"Oh, that is only the beginning of it," said the purser. "You know there is always a boy on night-watch, walking through the gangways to see there isn't any sneak-thieving going on; but, if you can believe it, from the night we left San Francisco the boys seem to have arranged among themselves to stand an extra watch in the little passageway where Mrs. Potwin's cabin is, as if they were afraid something might happen to her. We have to do that sort of thing sometimes, when a passenger has a touch of jim-jams, but as for its being done without any orders, in a sly kind of a way, it's unheard-of. I tell you I believe that the whole steward's crew are so devoted to that woman that if he gave them one order and she gave them another they would do what she said. And it isn't only in the saloon either. I saw her down on the steerage-deck the other morning giving cakes to the children, and all the Japanese down there seemed to

be afraid of her. She has never been to
Japan in her life, and I don't know what
there is about her, but they all seem to think
that she is some sort of a high cockalorum.
I can't make head or tail of it."

"Why don't you ask her?" said I. "She
must have noticed it."

"Of course she's noticed it," said the
purser; "and what's more, she takes it as
a matter of course; and more than that, she
expects it. Now I'll tell you another funny
thing. As I was going on deck the other
morning she was standing at the head of the
companionway; one of the Japanese boys
was speaking to her, and just as I came up
he must have said something she didn't
like, for she flashed out with one of those
funny little quick tempers of hers, and said
a Japanese word to him. It was a word
I'd never heard before, but I know it was
Japanese. I can't remember now what
the word was, but I asked my own boy that
night what it meant, of course without saying where I had heard it, and I could not
get any satisfaction out of him. He mut-
tered something about not understanding,

and has been looking sulky ever since. And the strangest part of the business is that she can't speak Japanese at all, though she seems to want to learn. I taught her how to say *kudasai* and *arigato* and 'How do you do' and 'Good-by' and a few other little things like that, and it didn't seem to come easy to her. I've been kicking myself ever since for having forgotten that word she said to the boy. I know I can talk Japanese as well as the ordinary foreigner, but I don't know any word that will knock a man as cold as that did."

"Surely," said I, "if you think there is anything mysterious about all this, which seems to me to be a mere series of unimportant coincidences, you might ask her. You are certainly not afraid of her; on the contrary, you and she are good friends, and she couldn't strike you to the earth by aiming her terrible Japanese word at you, for you don't know what it means. I'd ask her that, before anything else, if I were you."

The purser put fresh ice in his glass, and then, looking around the room as if he imagined Mrs. Potwin might be hidden behind a curtain, ready to hurl the dreadful word, said :

"Between you and me, I'm afraid to."

"Afraid!" said I ; "surely that is too absurd."

"Don't you be too cocksure of that," rejoined the purser. "I've been in Japan and China a good deal more than you have, and I tell you that there are a good many things it's dangerous for a foreigner to meddle with."

"But she is a foreigner herself," I objected.

"She is and she isn't," said the purser. "I believe she's never been to Japan before, and I believe she doesn't know a dozen words of Japanese ; but the Japanese don't treat her as a foreigner. As far as you and I can see she's only a jolly young grass-widow making a trip around the world ; but you take my word for it there is something out of the ordinary going on, and I'll be mighty glad when she's off the ship."

"But what harm can she do?" said I. "You don't mean to be preposterous enough to tell me that she has come on board to raise mutiny, seize the steamer, and set up in business as a female pirate?"

"No, I don't think that," said he, "and I don't know but what I am more afraid of harm coming to her than to anybody else on board. The chief steward and I were talking it over yesterday, and he thinks the reason they all seem to be devoted to her is because they're afraid of her."

"Perhaps they think she has the evil eye," I suggested. "I don't remember hearing that they have a superstition of that sort in Japan, but it may be so. I can't believe you are really afraid to speak to her about it, although I can understand that, as you have an official position on board the ship, you might feel awkward about it. But I don't in the least mind asking her why it is that the Japanese boys take so much more trouble for her than they do for the rest of us. I remember, now you speak of it, that I have noticed it myself, and I see no reason why I should not ask her."

"If you take my tip," said the purser, "in the first place, you won't mix yourself up in the business at all, won't say anything about it to her; and, in the second place, if you do speak to her about it, take mighty good care there isn't one of the Japanese within ear-shot when you do. Whether they are stewards or sailors or anything else, there always seems to be some one of them who finds an excuse to have some little job to do around where she is, whether she is in the saloon or on deck. They are the mildest, pleasantest people in the world, the Japs, take them all around, but queer things happen sometimes. Aboard one of the other boats of the line they had a French passenger one trip who had been obliged to leave Nagasaki because he had maltreated a Japanese girl there, and one moonlight night when he was leaning over the stern somebody must have tipped up his heels, for another passenger who had left him standing there a few minutes before found him missing when he came back. There was no reason to believe that he had committed suicide either."

" If there is any danger of that sort in store for me I must persuade Mrs. Potwin to teach me the necromantic word, and then if

one of the enchanted stewards tries to throw
me overboard from your spellbound steamer I can wither him on the spot," said I.
"And now I think I will go up and get a
breath of air before I turn in."

It was nearly midnight, but I found Mrs.
Potwin sitting in her deck-chair, with one of
the enamoured youths of the smoking-room
elongated at her side, and when I approached she bade him go away and leave me his
chair. He obeyed her with shame-faced
docility, and as I spread his rug over my
knees, I asked her why she was not below
in her cabin.

"Because it distresses the missionaries'
wives when I stay on deck after eleven
o'clock, and I like it up here in the moonlight anyway."

"But what have the missionaries' wives
done to you? They are very worthy people
in their way, and I don't see why you want
to shock them."

"Oh, I do it on principle, just as I wear
short sleeves in the morning. Women always make themselves disagreeable to me,
and I always make myself disagreeable to

women. It has been that way ever since I
was a little girl, and I am a perverse child
still, you see. I have a big doll down in my
steamer-trunk now. I never go anywhere
without it. And some evening when I want
to tease the missionaries' wives very badly,
I'm going to bring it out in the saloon and
play with it. You see, I'm only nineteen,
and I don't look more than sixteen, so I
have a right to do silly things like that if I
want to."

"You might occupy your time more prof-
itably," said I. "Why don't you try to
learn a little Japanese? You would find
the country much more interesting if you
understood the language."

"It won't take me long to pick it up once
I'm there," she replied. "I can learn a
language easily enough if I can hear people
talking it, but I hate to study it out of a
book."

I thought I had made my opportunity
then, and was on the point of asking her
about the wonderful Japanese word, when I
saw one of the stewards standing outside
the chart-room, well within ear-shot of us;

and, although I was half ashamed to pay
any heed to the purser's caution, I thought
I would wait to put my question until we
were quite alone. I knew, too, that it would
be a long story, if she told me anything at
all, and I didn't want to stay on deck until
two o'clock in the morning, even for the
sake of scandalizing the missionaries' wives.
So, after I had let her talk about nothing at
all for a little while, I went below, leaving
her alone in her chair with the moonlight
shining full on her yellow hair, and the Japanese boy standing near, like a little wood-
en soldier on sentry duty.

III

The pleasures of life are not so hot or so
frequent that one can afford to treat lightly
the promise of their coming, and I prepared
myself to hear the story which I knew
Ysonde Potwin had to tell as thoughtfully
as an epicure prepares himself for a feast.
For a whole day I let her severely alone,
knowing that her theory of life was one of

oscillation, and that she would be the more friendly and confidential the day after my abstention. And when the time came, and our chairs extended themselves side by side in a remote corner of the deck, I asked her, direct enough, why all the Japanese on board made so much fuss about her.

"Oh, I can't tell you that!" she exclaimed. "It's a secret, and you know women love secrets!"

"Yes, they love secrets as much as they love their rings," I replied. "But if you keep your diamonds shut up in a little tin box at your banker's, you get no joy out of them; and if you don't tell your secrets, you might as well not have any."

"Oh, it wouldn't make you like me any better if I told you," she said.

"I don't believe the secret is as black as that," I replied. "You know I told you, long ago, that I was too lazy to lose my heart to you, as those other fellows do, and you said we would be frank and loyal ship-mates. And if you have secrets from me, I shall hide all sorts of thrilling and tremu-

lous mysteries from you, and see what a loss
that would be all around."

"Well," said she, "I suppose I must tell
you. It would be rather a relief to tell
somebody, and no one knows about it, not
even my maid. I'll tell you all about it;
but if I find you don't like me any more,
and neglect me the rest of the voyage as
you did yesterday, it will be real mean of
you."

Playing with the rings on her soft white
fingers, and looking out over the silvered
waves of the summer sea, she told me the
story of Temehichi.

"Once upon a time, to begin with, I was
divorced. I told you that before. And
Mr. Potwin went off to Europe or somewhere; and that's the end of him. And I
couldn't go to Europe or anywhere, because
it was in May, and I had given the lawyers
nearly all my money, and I wasn't going to
have any more till October. So I took a
little flat in San Francisco, and I lived there
alone with old Delia, who is here with me
now, and whom I am going to send back
to America as soon as we get to Japan, and

who has been with me ever since I was a
little girl, and who is the dearest old woman
in the world, only that she will drink too
much, sometimes; and when she drinks too
much she keens all night because her friends
in Ireland are dead. And Delia got an
Irish girl to do the house-work and to cook
my breakfast in the morning. I always
used to go out for lunch and for dinner, it
was so much brighter and gayer in the restaurants than being alone at home. Delia
and the Irish girl quarrelled about Home-
Rule, and I got a Swedish girl. She stamped
about like a cart-horse, and broke everything she touched, and I couldn't have her
any more. So I thought I'd try a Japanese
boy. You know we have a great many
Japanese and Chinese boys for servants in
San Francisco, more Chinese than Japanese, but this was a Japanese boy. They're
always called boys, but they're grown up,
you know. He was very quiet and very
quick, and got his work done in no time at
all; and he used to sit in the little kitchen
and write letters all day; and he was always out at night, nearly. It didn't make

any difference to me, as long as his work was done ; but Delia used to hear him come in at five o'clock in the morning. She told him once that if he didn't sleep more he'd be sick and die ; and he told her people had different ways of sleeping, and that he slept while he was cleaning up the flat. He made beautiful buckwheat cakes, and he didn't care a cent if I had my breakfast one morning at nine o'clock and the next morning at eleven ; he never complained the least little bit, and everything was as nice as could be. And one afternoon Charley Hart came to take me down to the Maison Riche for dinner. You know the Maison Riche is one of the French restaurants in San Francisco, and Charley Hart was a great friend of mine. He is in the insurance business, and he plays the banjo splendidly, and he belongs to one of the clubs, and he is a great society man. Well, it was raining so hard that I thought it would be fun to send a messenger-boy out and have something brought in from a restaurant, and have our dinner there. So I told Temehichi—Temehichi was the Japan-

10

ese boy's name—to call a district messenger and order enough for two. Temehichi
asked me what time I wanted it, and I told
him in about an hour. We had a lovely
dinner, and I found out afterwards that instead of having things from a restaurant,
Temehichi had cooked it all himself. He
was the handiest human being I ever saw ;
he could just do anything ; so after that,
when I was alone, I often used to have my
meals at the flat instead of going out; and
every one who came to see me said there
never was such a boy as Temehichi. You
see, I have a lot of gentlemen friends in
San Francisco. They used to be Mr. Potwin's friends, but they all took my side
about the divorce, and they used to come
to see me all the time. But Charley Hart
came oftener than any of the others. If you
knew anything about San Francisco you'd
understand it better, because everybody
there knows him. You see, he is such a
society favorite, and yet he is lonesome,
after all. He always leads the german everywhere ; and when any of the rich people
want to give a big party, they get Charley

to come and arrange everything. He knows
whom to ask and whom to leave out, and
all about ordering the supper and the mu-
sic; and he has had lots of lovely things
given him by people he has been nice to in
that way. One of them gave him an ele-
gant gold watch with his monogram on it in
diamonds. And when a young lady first
goes into society in San Francisco, if he
isn't on her side she can't do anything at
all. He is asked out to dine nearly every
night, and of course it all helps him in his
business, because he is agent for both life
and fire companies, and lots of people who
are trying to get into society do their insur-
ing through him. Well, everybody thinks
he has such a lovely time, but he isn't so
very happy, after all. He is nearly forty
now; and last fall he began to get so fat
that it was awful for him to have to dance.
But of course it wouldn't do for him not to
dance, so he had to go without eating lots
of things he likes. And whenever there
happened to be an evening when he wasn't
asked to a dinner-party anywhere, it was
awfully stupid for him, because he hasn't

any real friends—they are all society friends
—so he got into the way of coming to see
me a great deal. We would go to dine together somewhere, and perhaps go to the
theatre afterwards. He can always have
seats at any theatre he wants, because the
managers like to have him go to see all the
new attractions, he's such a society man.
And then, after the theatre, we would go up
on the car together to my flat, and sit down
and eat pickled limes and lady-fingers :
that's about the only thing he can eat for
supper. And then he would sit and play on
the banjo, and tell me what he had been
doing the night before, for ever so long. Of
course going to so many parties he had got
into the way of staying up late, and I never
used to think anything of his being there
till one o'clock.

"One Monday about three months ago
one of the most prominent men in San Francisco died, and it just so happened that
different people who were going to give parties or have companies to dinner Tuesday,
Wednesday, and Thursday were all distant
relations of his, or else were so much con-

"HE WOULD SIT AND PLAY ON THE BANJO"

nected with him in their business, through
the railroad or something like that, that everything had to be postponed, and there
were hardly any theatre parties either. So
that all Charley's engagements were broken
off; and instead of only getting orchestra
seats, he had proscenium boxes given to him
for two different theatres—one for Tuesday
night and one for Wednesday night. We
went out to dinner together both nights,
and then to the theatre afterwards; and
Thursday night I said I was tired going out,
and I got Temehichi to cook dinner for us
at the flat. And Charley brought up a lot
of new songs, and after dinner he played
his banjo and I played my hired upright,
and we sang and had lots of fun, and he
stayed awfully late. I told him he was silly
not to go home, because he was at so many
parties he ought to be glad to go to bed
early when he got the chance. But he said
he wasn't a bit sleepy, and I don't know
what time it was when he went home at
last; but it was ridiculous of him to stay so
long, anyhow. When I went to let him out,
I saw that the kitchen door was ajar and

the gas was burning; so I knew Temehichi, instead of going out that night, must have stayed there writing his letters. I went to bed, humming over to myself one of the songs Charley and I had been learning. I should think I must have been asleep about an hour before I heard a noise in my room that woke me up. I always turn the gas down low when I go to bed, but it was turned on full now, and there in the middle of the room, right near the corner of my bed, stood Temehichi, dressed in a magnificent Japanese costume, embroidered all over with dragons and snakes. And fastened in his belt there were two curved scabbards for swords, but the swords were not in them. He had one in each hand—great, long, crooked swords. He looked just like one of the pictures of ancient Japanese soldiers that you see on a fan. At first I thought I must be dreaming, and I was noticing how beautifully his things were embroidered, when he took a step nearer to me, and said :

" '*You bad woman ; now you die !*'

" It was so much like a crazy kind of a

dream that at first I wasn't frightened at
all. If a man had come in there with a
revolver, I suppose I'd have screamed;
but this was so different from anything I
ever thought could happen to me, that I
couldn't realize it enough to be scared. I
didn't say anything—just lay there without
taking my head off the pillow, and he said
over again, very slowly:

"' *You bad woman; now you die!*'

"And he rattled together the two swords
like a man sharpening knives. That woke
me up more, but I didn't say a word; I just
looked at him in a stupid kind of way,
thinking all the while how cute his Japanese things were. Then he made a long
speech, not in as good English as he used
to speak when he wasn't excited, and his
eyes looked as if he were out of his head,
but every other way he was quiet enough,
only you could see he was awfully angry.
I can remember every word of it, nearly,
just the way he said it.

"' Yes, you bad woman,' he began. ' I
thought you good woman, but to-night your
Charley-dog he stay too late. You think

I only a common servant - boy, you bad
woman! Now I tell you who I am. My
people all *daimio*, what you call princes. I
belong Tokugawa family. Tokugawa Iye-
yasu was my fifteen times grandfather, and
he was *shogun*, what you call king, three
hundred years before now. All my people
kings or brothers of kings. Then you born.
Very year you born everything in Japan
change. Just to-day I ask Delia how old
you are — you born same day Tokugawa
soldiers lose Wakamatsu Castle. Since
that war all Japan change — no more *shoguns* now; all government different. Hundred years ago, priests say some day beautiful white bird be born with Gold Beak,
and that day Tokugawa kings end. You
that bird with Gold Beak — bad woman!
When you born you bring trouble my
people — but that not enough for you —
Gold Beak! You listen: I speak your
dog-English very slow — I remember all I
learn at school. Tokugawa people great
people, every way — great when they fight,
great when they make *uta* poems, great
when they try to learn. Now I speak slow,

like a dog- English book, and you listen
every word I say — for you never hear anybody else talk any more. Listen, Gold Beak
— listen both your ears! My grandfather
was not *shogun*—*shogun's* brother, and when
revolution come he was killed, and my
father had to go north—what we call Yezo
— very wild island, where very poor wild
people live — what we call Ainos — people
all hairy like bears, and very cruel. My
father so kind, so good, so brave, all the
Ainos learn to love him, and he live there
quiet. For long time I was hidden — for I
was born wartime, Gold Beak, three months
before you, and my mother was afraid Satsuma people kill me if they find me. But
by-and-by my father send for me to come
to him in Yezo—and he bring me up to be
strong. He teach me to use a sword, he
give me these swords here, swords of my
family, same swords that will now cut off
head of Bird with Golden Beak. When I
am older my father say to me: " *You see
that mountain, Komaga-take, all snow, snow
up to shoulders? Our family is like that
mountain—under snow. The mikado sees the*

snow, and he says: 'Very cold, very cold!
Tokugawa people all under snow — like last
spring cherry blossoms.' Then he laughs.
But look again, my boy. If you go up through
snow to top of mountain, you find there small
ponds of boiling water, and if you step too
hard the ground gives way, and you go through
where all inside mountain is fire. Sometimes
top of mountain opens, and hot stones and all
hot things fly out, and the snow is all steam, and
people in villages at the foot of the mountain—
who laugh when they look at the snow—are
all killed. Tokugawa family same way: we
lie cold now, snow over us, but still have fire
at heart — and some day the mikado and the
Satsuma people and the Choshiu people and
the Tosa people all find the snow can change to
steam very quick—and they see old Tokugawa
swords swing again. But you must learn, my
boy. Japan is full of new ways — European
ways—dog-ways. I hate those ways, and you
must hate them—but you must learn them. I
am going to send you far from Japan, where
you learn a new language — dog-language—
where you learn all the Choshiu and the Satsuma people learn; and when you have learned

*all this—you and all the others who had dai-
mio fathers — some day there come another
war, and some day another Tokugawa shogun
have Japan."*

"'That is how my father talked to me,
Golden - Beak — that is why I came to
America. I came alone with one servant—
his grandfathers had been servants of my
grandfathers for three hundred years. I
went to your schools, I learned your dog-
language. I can speak your English when
I speak slowly — plenty of it. But you die
— bad woman! We are all alone — I tell
you all my story very slowly — so you see I
can speak your English. After the schools
I go to Washington. I study law, to learn
how English laws, American laws, dog-laws,
are made—and then I had no more money,
and my father was dead. But I wanted not
to go back to Japan. I wanted to learn
more; I said I stay here until I go back
with my two swords in my hands. I left
Washington; I come here San Francisco.
I find it very hard to live here. My old
servant could carve out of the wood, and he
carve the wood to keep us alive, then he

die. Now listen—bad woman! You think
because I am your servant that I am nothing here. You say: " In Japan maybe so
his people great people — but here he no
money, no friends—he nobody." Big mistake, Golden-Beak — big mistake. I have
friends, good many hundreds, Japanese
friends, who love me and believe in me—
and believe that before my hair is gray I
perhaps be *shogun*. We are a few hundreds
in your dog-town here, together in a club—
we are many thousands in Japan. We don't
speak yet—we only whisper. But some day
we speak, and all Japan will hear—mikado
will hear—Satsuma people will hear—all
will hear—and *shoguns* will rule Japan again.
All those others in this club here, they poor
boys like me—but in Japan we have for our
side people who have some money left,
after the mikado and the Choshiu people
and the Tosa people and the Satsuma people have robbed them. They still have
money, and they offer me money. They
say: " Sons of Tokugawa no work like
coolies ; you must not sweep a floor — we
give you all you need." I say : " No. A

son of Tokugawa will sweep a floor, but no son of Tokugawa will let you give him food when he is poor. When he is a great man, then, yes, you shall give it to him, and he will have it; but now—never!" So you see, Golden - Beak, I sweep your floor, I clean the mat where dog-Charley wipes his feet — and you laugh. You laugh, all of you. You say: "Oh, very clean; oh, very good boy." But the snow is only on the skin of Komaga-take. When Charley-dog have dinner here, I spit in his soup. You think I am a broom; you think I am an iron to stir the fire with; but all the while I am a man, Golden-Beak, and all the while you are a woman. And I love you, bad woman! One day you left your door open —I see you with your hair all down your breast, and I see your breast under your hair —bad woman! After that I often stand at your door. I think you know it all the time —bad woman! I think you laugh; I think you say: "Poor Japanese boy, he look at me; he may look—he not a man, he only a broom, an iron to stir the fire with." And every time I look I love you more, bad woman! And now it is Charley-dog who looks at your hair all down your breast, and you no laugh at him. I know, Golden-Beak, he stay too late to-night. And now you die! I think you don't have much religion, even your dog-religion. You sleep all the Sunday morning, you don't go to church. But all you dog-Christians very religious when you going to die. If you want to be religious now — bad woman !— you make a prayer; you never make an-other.'

" That was what the boy said to me, stand-ing there dressed in the embroidered robes of a Japanese nobleman, and with his two swords in his hands. Of course I was scared. Anybody would have been, let alone me. But as soon as the boy told me that he was in love with me, and I remembered that I sometimes had seen him hanging around my door, I wasn't so much scared. When a man is in love with you he's a fool. That is what I always think. He will threaten to murder you, and he will do all sorts of awful things, but you can manage him. And I was sure that I could manage Temchichi.

I told him he must be crazy. I told him
that Charley Hart and I were very good
friends, and that was all; and that if Charley had stayed later than usual that night,
it was only because we had a lot of new
songs to learn. And I told him that if he
was to be a great man and a great soldier,
it was a poor way for him to begin by kill-
ing a helpless woman. And I told him that
he ought to have let me know his story
long before, and have let me try to be his
friend. He stood quite still for a long time,
looking at the blue edges of the swords, and
then he said to me :

"'Bad woman, if I let you live, would
you try to be good?'

"I said I didn't think I had been very
bad, but that of course I would try to be
good if he would not murder me.

"'After you have got to be a good woman,
will you love me?' said he.

"I told him that I didn't know, that he
couldn't expect to make me love him by
threatening to chop my head off, that he
must wait and see.

"Finally he said he would not kill me

that night, he would wait, and that if I
would be a good woman he would marry
me, and when he went back to Japan, and
the revolution came, and he was a great
man, I should be his wife. And he told me
that he knew he was doing wrong, that it
had been his father's idea that when the
new government was established all foreigners should be driven out of Japan, and that
for him to have a foreign consort when he
was made *shogun* would be very inconsistent.
But he hoped, he said, that if I tried hard I
could grow to become almost like a Japanese. Then he made me a low bow, put his
swords back in his scabbards, and marched
out of the room.

"When I got up the next morning he
cooked my breakfast for me as usual, and
then I went down to Charley Hart's office
to ask him what I had better do. He was
awfully frightened, and said that if I didn't
complain to the police and have Temehichi
locked up we would both probably be killed.
But I told him that I couldn't do that—that
it would make an awful scandal, and people
would say all sorts of things about me and

about him, and that anyhow I wouldn't do
it. I said that as long as I didn't allow my
friends to stay too late in the evening, I
didn't believe the boy would murder me or
give me any more trouble, and that it was
all his fault for having stayed so late, anyway. Charley said :

" ' All right, have your own way about it;
but I am never going up to your flat again
while you have that raving maniac there.'

" And he didn't ; he was frightened nearly to death. Well, for a menth or so Temehichi never said a word to me except about
his work. I didn't know whether to believe
his story or to think that he was out of his
head. And about that time I began to get
awfully tired of San Francisco. I had given
one of my friends who was on the Stock
Exchange three hundred and fifty dollars to
speculate with for me, and he had been so
lucky with it that I made up my mind that
I would go off to Europe. Then I thought
how much I would like to take a trip around
the world, and I thought that if I went by
the way of Japan I would stop there for a
while, and see what kind of a place it was.

11

I sort of half believed what Temehichi had told me. It sounded kind of crazy, but with his Japanese dress and his swords and all that, he really seemed to be somebody very wonderful. And, anyhow, I thought I would speak to him about it. So one morning I told him that I had made up my mind to go to Japan and see what kind of a country it was, and see if I would like to live there, and that in the meantime he and his friends could go on getting ready their revolution. Then he asked me if I really loved him, and was going to marry him, and I told him it was too early to talk about that, because I didn't know until I had seen Japan whether I could turn myself into a Japanese or not. He said that when I got to Japan the members of his Reactionary Society would do everything in the world for me, and that I should see what a lot of power he really had. Of course I don't know how much of all his talk is nonsense, but, anyhow, I know that all the Japanese on the steamer are as sweet as pie to me, and wait on me hand and foot. The only thing I don't like about it is that he seems to have arranged things so that I

"'I DON'T KNOW ANYTHING ABOUT THAT,'
REPLIED MRS. POTWIN"

can't talk to a man five minutes without one of his Japanese coming sneaking up to see what is going on."

" But surely," said I, " my dear Mrs. Potwin, you don't mean to tell me that every Jap on the ship belongs to this wonderful society, and takes his orders from your friend Temehichi?"

" I don't know anything about that," replied Mrs. Potwin, " but perhaps those who are not in it are afraid of those who are—and that is why it is that they all look after me so much."

This, then, was the secret which had perplexed the purser, and as I said good-night to Mrs. Potwin, I had an eye over my shoulder to see if any of the Japanese were watching us. But so far as I could see we were not observed.

The whole story was wild and fantastic, and yet I couldn't for the moment make up my mind altogether to disbelieve it. I was, at any rate, enough interested to wonder very much what the Beautiful Bird with the Golden Beak would do in Japan.

IV

The morning after Mrs. Potwin had told me the story of Temehichi, the purser called me into his office as I rose from the break-fast-table and said:

"Well, did you pump Mrs. Potwin last night? You had her in a corner long enough."

"I did my best," I replied, "and she talked about all sorts of things, but I failed to learn the mysterious Japanese word. I wish I knew it. It would be as good as a railway pass or a cart-load of money all through Japan."

"I suppose that is as much as to say that you know all about it, but had to promise to keep your mouth shut," said the purser. "Well, we have only got a few more days to Yokohama, and I hope there will be no bedevilments in the meantime."

Mr. Chamberlain's prayer was answered, for nothing more tremendous than one or two quarrels among the young men of the smoking-room disturbed the latter days of

the passage. Then there began to be a
great stirring about, and the steerage passengers were busily engaged in dropping
many-colored fragments of paper and little
handfuls of rice into the sea, seeking to
propitiate the gods, and praying that they
might find their friends in safety, and pros-
per in their undertakings. A noisy gull
came out to show us the way to the bar at
Yokokama, and early the next morning the
chain was rattling from the hawse-hole, and
the white dome of Fuji-san loomed vaguely
through the clouds.

I had Mrs. Potwin somewhat on my conscience. I did not want to bear her ashore
with me like a bird of brilliant plumage I
had killed at sea, and yet it would be heartless to leave her to the mercy of the boatmen
and the hotel runners. And she seemed to
me a pitiful little figure, arriving there in a
strange country, with her bright blue eyes
and her bright yellow hair, to involve herself in I knew not what plots and intrigues.
I had made a good many English friends
when I had been in Japan before, and there
is a pleasant little knot of exiles living on

the Bluff beyond the town always very ready
to be kind to strangers. But I couldn't
quite see myself asking Mrs. This or Mrs.
That to call on a "Mrs. Potwin, an American lady whose acquaintance I had made on
board the steamer." I could have warned
them that her gowns were very surprising,
and that her manners were very American.
But there would be more than that to explain. English people, even if they are living
at the world's end, entertain a belief, and
perhaps not an altogether mistaken one,
that young ladies whose marriages have mis-
carried should not travel about the world
without the protection of some older woman
whose life has been more commonplace.
And it never seemed to enter Mrs. Potwin's
head that her drunken Irish maid was not a
sufficient chaperon.

I learned long ago that it is always foolish
for a man to try to help any woman about
her social position, even in the miscellaneous
society of a minor colony. A woman who
is herself in a good position can, if she becomes interested in an eccentric creature
like Mrs. Potwin, do a great deal to set her

afloat; but the mere fact that a man is trying to help a woman in that way gives her
a black eye at the outset. And, after all,
English people who are living in out-of-the-
way corners of the world have very good
reason to be more suspicious than people
at home. Every woman's first instinct when
she finds that she is being talked about is
to go somewhere where no one has ever
heard of her. A man may do the same
thing, but it is infinitely easier to know
when a man is wrong. If he has been
caught cheating at cards in England, it is a
moral certainty that he cannot go to a colonial club more than three or four times
without encountering some one who knows
all about him. Men travel about more than
women, and the gossips of the outlying clubs
manage to keep themselves very well posted about the happenings in the clubs at
home. An undesirable traveller may sometimes be given the freedom of a colonial
club by a too confiding acquaintance, but
he never lasts long. With women it is a
very different matter. As long as a woman
doesn't pretend to be anybody extraordi-

narily smart, it is by no means so simple a
matter to trace her antecedents, and this
tends to make people more cautious. I
knew, too, apart from all these general
principles, that if I induced any one I knew
in Yokohama to give Mrs. Potwin the freedom of the Bluff, she would inevitably flirt
with all the men and set all the women by
the ears. Plainly enough it was the path
of wisdom for me to let her shift for herself from the start.

On the whole I was not a little relieved
when a very respectable young Japanese
came out to us on the health officer's
launch and told Mrs. Potwin that he had
been asked by friends in California to do
what he could to be of use to her. Directed
by him, she went to the hotel which I had
selected for myself, but I did not see her
again that night, as I was dining at the
club. The next day she told me that she
had made up her mind to try the experi-
ment of taking a little Japanese house for
a month or two, and living altogether in
the Japanese fashion. I told her that she
must let me go and ask her for a cup of tea

when she had settled herself, and she said that she would make an exception in my favor, although she had resolved to have nothing to do with the European colony. So I no longer had to trouble myself about trying to find some one to be kind to her, and for a fortnight I only saw her once or twice, and then when she was flying through the streets in a very smart jinrikisha, with two excellent runners.

I was amusing myself very well, but still I was pleased when one day I found a little note from her at the club to tell me that she had made her home in one of the Japanese quarters, half-way up the hill, and asking me to come and eat a Japanese dinner with her that night. I had travelled enough in the interior of Japan to be quite able to eat native food when nothing else was to be had, but I must have liked Mrs. Potwin very much to have been willing to put up with that sort of fare in Yokohama. At any rate, she did it all uncommonly well. She had three or four Japanese maids, much prettier than one usually sees anywhere but in a tea-house, and her little home was furnished in the very best Japanese taste. I had to drink tea and *saki*, and I had to eat raw fish, and everything was flavored with the inexhaustible *soy*. Mrs. Potwin herself was exquisitely dressed in the Japanese fashion, and had already learned the rudiments of Japanese etiquette. It was, of course, absurd to see so fair-haired and fair-skinned an American woman masquerading as a Japanese, but she was a little creature, and the dress looked better on her than it ever does on a foreign woman of ordinary stature. After dinner she played her *samisen* for me, and told me how much in earnest she was about adopting Japanese manners and customs. She was in the first flush of that enthusiasm which Japan always excites in a stranger, and sat cross-legged on her mat with heroic perseverance. I asked her what she had heard from Temehichi, and she told me she had only received one short letter, but that his friends in Yokohama had shown every wish to be of service to her, and had taken a great deal of trouble to install her comfortably in her Japanese abode.

"HER LITTLE HOME WAS FURNISHED IN THE BEST JAPANESE TASTE"

in San Francisco, people say, and the Europeans learn it from the Chinese. Perhaps your friend the Japanese boy took to the habit, and it has affected his head. I won't say positively that I know he can't be of the great Tokugawa clan, because the Europeans to whom I have talked take no interest at all in the descendants of a fallen dynasty, and the Japanese themselves are very shy of talking about the Tokugawa people. You see the affair of 'sixty-eight isn't a mere episode in the history of Japan. It is still so recent an event that the Japanese don't like to talk about it. But I have my doubts all the same. And I can't understand all that stuff about his using the two swords. So far as I can make out, the *daimio* and the *samurai* classes used to wear two swords, partly for show, and partly to have a spare weapon in reserve, but I don't believe they ever used them both."

"I don't call that any argument," said Mrs. Potwin. "Poor Temehichi might very easily have got muddled about a little detail like that. According to his own story, he wasn't born until the old customs were all

done away with, and he may have mixed
up what his father taught him."

"It's a queer business altogether," said
I, "and the queerest part of it all is that I
can't quite make up my own mind what to
believe and what not to believe. I have
asked one or two very well-informed men
here about the political situation of the
country, of course without saying a word
about this extraordinary story of yours, and
from what they tell me there is nothing less
likely than even an unsuccessful insurrection, let alone an accomplished revolution.
There have been one or two little disturb-
ances since the establishment of the mikado's government, but there is no serious
political party in Japan which wants to re-
store the old order of things. I asked one
of these men whether he believed there
were any revolutionary or reactionary soci-
eties at work, and he told me that, although
there might be some small associations of
ambitious and hare-brained young men,
there was certainly no organization of any
importance."

"Well," said Mrs. Potwin, "if you believe

that, I don't see how you are to explain what I have seen with my own eyes, and what you have seen too, for that matter. How could a poor Japanese servant-boy like Temehichi get the stewards on board the steamer to take so much trouble about me, and how could he have friends here to do all sorts of things for me unless they all belonged to some secret society?"

"I know," said I, "that I can't account for what happened on board the steamer, but it is easy enough to explain what you have seen here in Yokohama. He writes to some man here he knows, saying you are going to hire a house and buy a lot of Japanese things, and of course the shopkeepers, and the people who get a commission from the shopkeepers for bringing customers to them, are all very glad to help you find what you want."

"But there is more than that to be explained," said Mrs. Potwin. "It isn't only in the way of helping me to buy things that these people have been kind to me. They pay me all sorts of little attentions, and everything is made as easy as can be for me.

I don't say that I really believe there will ever be another *shogun* in Japan, and they may have to wait for years and years before they even try to get up a revolution, but I am quite sure that Temehichi is more than an ordinary boy, and that there are a lot of people here ready to do anything he asks them to."

"If that is the case," said I, "it is quite clear to me that you are very unwise to have anything to do with them. You may be sure that the police in Japan, like the police in any other country, know pretty well everything there is going on in the way of agitation against the government, and that if these people are attempting anything of the sort they will all be brought up with a round turn one of these days, and if you mix yourself up with them it will be made uncommonly disagreeable for you at the same time."

"But the police can't do anything to me," said Mrs. Potwin. "No one here has said a word to me about any secret society or anything else of the kind. They come here to see me, and ask if they can be of any use.

One of them is a Japanese lawyer, and another is a clerk in one of the government offices at Tokio, who came all the way down here expressly to see me. They don't even mention Temehichi's name to me. They come and call on me, just so, and drink a great deal of tea out of very small cups, like anybody else, and want to know if they can do anything to make my stay in Yokohama more agreeable. There isn't anything out of the way about it. It is just as if I had come here with a lot of letters of introduction. Perhaps Temehichi hasn't anything at all to do with it; perhaps every stranger who comes and hires a little native house here is treated in the same way—how do I know? I never was in Japan before."

"As for other strangers being treated as you are," said I, "no one ever heard of an American lady, or a lady of any other country, coming here and making her home in the Japanese quarter, and living in Japanese fashion. However, it will be very good fun for you for a while, and you have certainly got a charming little house here and the prettiest maids I ever saw. I am going up-country, shooting for a month with a man, and I hope I will find you all right when I come back. In the meantime, if you should get yourself into any sort of trouble here, go to the American consul and tell him the whole story."

"All right," said she, "I will. But you needn't be anxious about me. And by the time you get back I shall be able to speak Japanese beautifully."

V

When I was a lad at school there were three or four excellent bathing-places indicated by the authorities; one in a shallow back-water for the smaller boys, and other more extensive reaches for those who had proved their ability to take care of themselves. But there were, I remember, not a few among us who used to sneak away to a muddy little bit of river where there were no diving-boards and no conveniences of any sort, because we thought that swimming ceased to be a pastime as soon as it was

12

recognized and organized as a part of our education. And it was not, perhaps, without some trace of our school-boy perversity that Frank Scarlett and I set out for a month's shooting in the northern part of the main island of Japan. Foreigners are not permitted to shoot over land more than ten miles from a treaty port, and it was only after chivvying the whole staff of the British Legation for a week that we succeeded in obtaining a special permission from the government, and even then we each had to keep a native policeman at our heels to explain to the country people that we were exalted beings, exempt from the customary restrictions. Scarlett, who is a keen sportsman and has excellent shooting of his own in England, would, I knew, be disgusted, but his obstinacy carried everything before it. He wanted to " do " Japan, and it was impossible for him to believe that he could see any new country without having a gun under his arm. We got a few deer, one lean and miserable boar, and very fair bags of duck and green pheasant, but we walked a *ri* for every head of game we saw. And

it is an extraordinary fact that all the geog-
raphers and all the makers of dictionaries
and guide-books are profoundly incapable
of translating any sort of foreign measure
into English. These wiseacres tell you that
a Japanese *ri* is two miles and a half in a
flat country and three miles and a half in
the hills, and expect you to be attended by
a surveying expedition in order that you
may ascertain with precision whether your
morning's walk lies over country hilly enough
to be measured by a long *ri* or flat enough
to be measured by a short *ri*. Scarlett and
I ultimately hit upon the expedient of counting every *ri* five miles and then dividing
each *ri* into ten whistling distances, for the
dogs we had borrowed in Yokohama were
always precisely half a mile away from
us. It was all very ridiculous as far as
the shooting went, but I killed time well
enough, for Scarlett had never been in
Japan before, and the agonies he suffered
in the native inns were to me vastly entertaining.

When we returned to Yokohama I took
him to see Mrs. Potwin. It seemed to me

that she was the nearest approach to anything genuinely Japanese which he could be expected to appreciate, and before he had known her a week it was plainly to be seen that he did appreciate her. I have laughed at not a few things in my life, but I have never seen anything so ridiculous as the wooing of Mrs. Ysonde Potwin, American *divorcée* and Japanese *fiancée*, by Sir Francis Scarlett. At the end of a fortnight he put a stop to my chaffing him, telling me that he meant to marry Mrs. Potwin if Mrs. Potwin would marry him, and that he hoped I would have the good taste if I had any comments to make to make them elsewhere than in his presence. He was old enough to take care of himself, or, at any rate, of such an age that he ought to have been able to take care of himself, but I could not help feeling that if I had not taken him to see her he would never have met her, and that I was in some degree responsible for his preposterous conduct. We came from the same county; his people had always been great friends of my people; and I had known, ever since we had been at school together,

that he was a fool.   As long as he confined
himself to the groove in which his late la-
mented father had set him running he did
very well.   He had plenty of money, and
did not throw it away.   His shooting in Nor-
folk cost him a good deal, but it was very
good shooting.   He always had two or three
horses in training, and they won him nearly
enough to pay for their keep.   He was by
no means the sort of man whom a card-
sharper would have selected as a likely vic-
tim.   But the moment he lost sight of his
customary social landmarks he was as helpless as a child astray on a moor.   There was
no reason that he should marry for some
years to come, and when the time came for
him to marry he ought to marry a woman
like one of my sisters or any other man's
sisters, not a woman who seemed to have
composed herself out of jumbled reminis-
cences of the cheap novels she had read.
But there he was, as much in earnest as any
man could be, and there was Ysonde Potwin,
charmed to have a second string to her
bow.   He took an infinite amount of trouble
to find better runners for his jinrikisha than

she had for hers—and hers were uncommonly good—and they used to run mad races every evening out beyond the cricket-ground, she in her Japanese dress, quite without head-gear, and her short yellow hair flying in the wind. They were like two children. I remembered her having told me on the steamer that she never travelled without a doll, and it seemed to me that Scarlett had set up a doll in his turn, and that she was the doll. They bought each other endless presents—for the most part wooden cooking utensils and Japanese artificers' tools they didn't know how to use. He had been a dull boy at school and an idle one, but she made him stick to his Japanese lessons until they could manage to keep up some kind of halting conversation. Then, to my horror, they announced that they were going off to Kioto together. I expostulated. I told Scarlett that she would of course get herself talked about if she went flying around the country with him without any chaperon; whereupon Scarlett told me that I was a low-minded beast, and that Japan was not England, and that

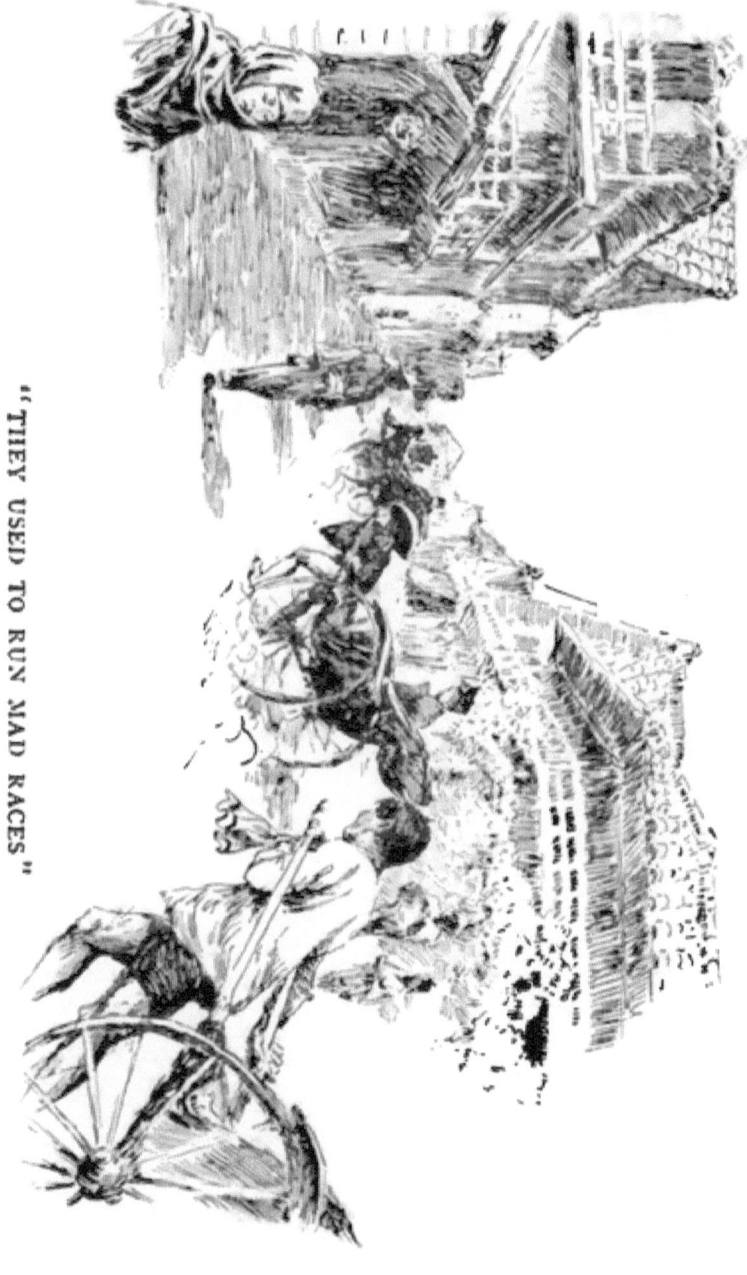

"THEY USED TO RUN MAD RACES"

American women were not English women, and that in America women were taught to take care of themselves, and that if I didn't think Mrs. Potwin knew how to take care of herself I had better not say so to him. I didn't want to come to blows with Scarlett, because I liked him, and because I thought it highly probable that he could punch my head several times before I could punch his once, so I addressed my remonstrances to the lady herself. She didn't lose her temper. She seemed to think it was a new and delightful sort of joke.

"If you knew," she said, "how much you look like my grandmother when you raise your eyebrows that way, you wouldn't do it. It's the simplest thing in the world, my friend. I am going to Kioto because I want to feed the carp at Kinkakuji. You'd go miles and miles to try to catch fish, and I have a mania for feeding fish. When I was three years old I used to take a globe full of goldfish to bed with me always. One person likes one kind of amusement, and another person likes another. And Frank is going to Kioto because he wants to shoot

the rapids of the Hozu. If he went all
the way to Aomori to shoot ducks, why
shouldn't he go to Kioto to shoot rapids?
I suppose you think I ought to wait till he
comes back to Yokohama before I go, or
let him wait till I come back before he
goes. That's your way of looking at it.
And you get your eyebrows away over to
the back of your head because I call him
Frank. If he were a man I had only seen
two or three times, you wouldn't be horrified at my going to Kioto because he happened to be going there, and yet you talk
about my going with Frank, who's quite an
old friend of mine now. Why, he's been
to see me every day for a month! Anyhow,
if you think it's so awful, why don't you
go along too? I'll tell everybody you are
my grandmother dressed up in a man's
clothes."

"Thank you very much for the invitation," said I, "but I think I won't go. Do
try to be serious for five minutes, won't
you? You know it's only because I like
you and take an interest in you that I
speak."

" I don't know whether it is or not," said
she. " I think you're half afraid Frank
and I will get married before we come
back. Why shouldn't I marry him, for that
matter? You are always talking about re-
spectability, and he's respectable, isn't he?"

" Yes," said I.

" And I'm not? What's the reason I'm
not? I'm divorced, but I divorced my
husband ; he didn't divorce me. Is it my
being engaged to Temehichi that makes it
so dreadful? Because if it is, I'm not engaged to him. He asked me to marry him,
and I told him I'd think about it. The
Queen of England couldn't give him a more
respectable answer than that, could she?
And as for Temehichi, he belongs to a very
old family, and he's awfully poor, and I
hear you and Frank say the same things
about lots of your friends in England."

" It is not your marrying Temehichi that
we are talking about," said I.

" And perhaps Temehichi is good enough
for me, but I'm not good enough for Sir
Francis Scarlett — I suppose that is what
you mean?" said the little woman.

" I mean that you will get yourself talked about if you go off to Kioto with him, after the way you two have been larking about Yokohama. That is what I mean," said I.

" And; if you please, who is going to talk about us?" asked Mrs. Potwin. " You! There isn't anybody else here who knows us both. So the worst of it is you'll have to talk to yourself. I can see you locking yourself up in a room and wagging your head at yourself and saying: ' Really, my dear fellow, it's a most shocking business,' and then agreeing with yourself that it is."

" Do you want to marry Scarlett ?" said I.

" One question deserves another," said Mrs. Potwin. " Do you think it would be a very hard thing for me to do if I did want to ?"

" I think, if you ask me," I replied, " that it would be easy enough for you to get married. I fancy that the consuls or the missionaries or some of those people are in the habit of marrying foreigners here. But as for the future, I am not sure that you wouldn't find it harder to turn yourself into an English woman and lead the life you would have to lead as Lady Scarlett, than to turn yourself into a Japanese woman and be the consort of a *shogun*."

"I don't know how that would be," she replied, "for I've never been to England; but I'll promise you one thing, if it will make your mind any easier: that if I do marry Frank, it won't be until after I have been over to his country and see how I like it."

"It is an original way of acquainting yourself with the various countries of the world," said I, "to engage yourself to men of one nationality after another, and make trial trips to their respective homes. Only you will have to draw the line somewhere, or you will be experimenting with a cannibal tribe one of these days, and have your pursuit of knowledge brought to an untimely end."

"You needn't worry about that," said she. "But, as you seem to be so worked up about it, I don't mind telling you one thing: that the man I marry will be either an Englishman or a Japanese."

"And you haven't made up your mind whether it is to be Scarlett or Temehichi?" I asked.

"If I have, I haven't told you," said Mrs. Potwin.

And I walked down the hill again to my hotel with no more definite information than that.

I saw them start on their journey, these two extraordinary young people. Their suite consisted of Scarlett's man, a native courier, and two of Mrs. Potwin's little Japanese maids. I saw the procession passing along the Bund on its way to the railway station, and Mrs. Potwin was kind enough to arrest the wild flight of her jinrikisha to bid me good-bye. I asked her why she was not taking a third maid with her, and also the little white donkey which I had bought for her one day, and which she sometimes used to drive in a cart. They might as well have a good big caravan while they are about it, I remarked. She told me that she hoped the two maids would chaperon one another, and that if she had taken the third maid she would also have needed a fourth to chaperon the third; as for the donkey, she didn't know what English manners and customs might be, but that American ladies considered it highly indecorous to travel about with a donkey. And with this parting jeer, off she went.

I heard of the party's movements from time to time, and I did not by any means find it necessary to talk to myself about them, as she had prophesied I should, for within a few days every man in the club knew about Scarlett's journey. An American woman whom nobody knows can do all sorts of eccentric things without arousing any one's interest or attention, but a man with a position in the world such as Scarlett enjoyed does not possess the same immunity. Every one seemed to know that Mrs. Potwin was a friend of mine, and I was heartily weary of being questioned about them before they came back to Yokohama—and they certainly did not hurry themselves. From Kioto they went all the way to Nikko, and from there both of them wrote to me. Scarlett said he was having a very good time, but that he still thought the

inns abominable, and that was about all he
had to say.

Mrs. Potwin was more communicative.
She said she had greatly enjoyed feeding
the fish at Kinkakuji, and that she had
gone to Nikko because she had heard that
the Japanese government was feeding the
fish with which Lake Chuzenji had been
stocked; and, as feeding fish was her great
object in life, she wanted to see how it was
being done. And Scarlett, she said, had
gone on to Nikko because, after shooting
the rapids of the Hozu, he wanted to see
the Daiyagawa. She hoped, she said, that
I would clearly understand that no affairs
of lesser moment would have induced them
to disturb my equanimity by travelling over
the same roads at the same time. And in
the meantime she was engaged to be married to Scarlett! It was not, she said, a
regular engagement: it was the species of
engagement called in America an "understanding"—a modified form of betrothal
which she considered exceedingly conven-
ient. She had told Scarlett that she was
"sort of half engaged" to somebody else,

IN THE FIELDS

and that, such being the case, she couldn't
accept him outright, but that if this other
conditional engagement should not result in
a permanent and binding engagement, she
would consider herself conditionally engaged to Scarlett. She didn't say what the
conditions of this doubly conditional engagement were, but it seemed, as far as I
could make it out, to be a solemn agree-
ment that they would marry one another if
they wanted to, and wouldn't marry one
another if they didn't want to. And in the
meanwhile, she said, she did not want to
have it "announced." This remarkable
letter ended with the statement that they
expected to be in Yokohama again at the
end of the month.

As a matter of fact, they didn't come back
at the end of the month, nor until half-way
through the next month. And when they
did come back, Scarlett told me in all seri-
ousness that Mrs. Potwin was going to
marry him, and that he thought she was
the sweetest, brightest, prettiest little woman he had ever seen, and that he was as
happy as could be, and that perhaps his

people at home wouldn't like it, but that he didn't care whether they liked it or not.

I offered him a cigar.

To ask him to smoke seemed a good, safe, conservative sort of thing to say, and I could not think of anything more definite that I thought it would be well to put into words.

He went on to tell me that he knew that in a great many respects Mrs. Potwin's ideas of life were different from the ideas of life entertained by our women at home; but that she was so sweet and so kind and so bright that he was sure she would get on with any sort of people anywhere in the world.

I gave him a match.

He next recited to me a long list of the names of Englishmen who had married Americans, and remarked that all of these American women had shown themselves pretty well able to hold their own in England, and that many of them had, for that matter, acquired no small degree of popularity in society.

I asked him to have a drink.

If he wanted any expression of opinion
from me, he was disappointed. I was determined that, if he crowded me into a corner and I had to say what I thought about
his projected marriage, that I would tell
him I thought him altogether out of his
mind ; but I preferred not to say so as long
as I could hold my peace.

But I talked to Mrs. Potwin. I told her
it was not a thing to be joked about ; that
Scarlett was a very honest fellow, and a
very kind fellow, and a very good fellow,
and a fellow I liked very much, and that he
seemed to have put it into her hands to
make him very unhappy if she saw fit so to
do. I told her frankly enough that I was
by no means sure that it lay equally in her
power to make him happy, and that, as for
her own chances of happiness, I thought
that England would be about the last place
in the world in which she would like to live.
Then I asked her what she had heard from
Temehichi. She showed me the last letter
she had received from him. It was quite
respectful and quite well expressed. It did
not allude to the Reactionary Society, and

13

it occupied itself chiefly with suggestions
for the furtherance of her health and comfort in Japan.   Apparently Temehichi had,
as yet, heard nothing about her flying about
with Scarlett, and he seemed to be quite at
peace with himself and with her.

Only a few days later, on Mrs. Potwin's
birthday, she received a strange sort of
present, which Temehichi must have had
made for her in Japan.   It was a little
bronze helmet, and was clamped upon the
head of a large French wax doll, which
came with it.   It entirely covered the head
of the doll, but was furnished with hinges
at one side; and, when a spring was touched
and the joint opened, the little helmet could
be removed.   The helmet itself was in the
form of a bird's head, the feathers being
simulated in white enamel.   The eyes were
two small garnets, and the bill, which was
shaped like that of a hawk, was made of
gold.   Mrs. Potwin was delighted with this
new toy, which was indeed most ingeniously
constructed and most exquisitely finished;
and it was a droll sight to see the doll, with
its pink cheeks and staring blue eyes, sud-

denly transformed into a mythic monster,
like the sun-god of the Nile, when its head
was covered by the casque. I didn't see
how Temehichi could have found the money
to pay for so elaborate a toy, but I was tired
of speculating about his mysteries. So far
as I knew she hadn't told Scarlett anything
about Temehichi, and I didn't think it was
my business to enlighten him. But she used,
when I found her alone, to put the helmet
on the doll, and, solemnly shaking her finger
at its golden beak, upbraid it after the manner of Temehichi, calling it " Gold Beak "
and " Bad Woman," a performance in which
she delighted.

Take it altogether, the little woman's
Japanese home was a pleasant place to go
for an hour or two, and I was sorry when
it was time for me to say good-bye to her.

VI

It was black March weather when I
found myself in England again, and it was
not until May that Scarlett came home. A

few days after I had heard of his return he
wrote to ask me to spend a week with him
at his place in Oxfordshire. I had made
up my mind to go up to town about the
time his letter came, but I am not one of
those men who cannot live unless they pass
the gates of St. James's Palace a certain
number of times every day for a certain
number of weeks in every year, and I love
the upper river. Scarlett's place is about
half-way between Oxford and Lechlade, on
the river-side, a great rambling old Eliza-
bethan house, without any such architect-
ural pretensions as to hinder his making it
thoroughly comfortable. Scarlett himself
came to meet me at Oxford, and told me as
we drove out that he had prevailed upon
several other men to impinge upon the
London season, and that he thought we
should have a very jolly time of it.

"And how did you leave Mrs. Potwin?" I asked him. "Is she still flying
up and down the Bund at Yokohama in
her 'rikisha?"

"I can't drive tandem and talk about
Mrs. Potwin at the same time," said Scar-

lett. "You shall hear all about her this evening." And then he talked horse — a subject which always bores me to death — until we turned into the long avenue of Dunkin House, just as the sunset was reddening the lustrous lily-pads in the river.

When I went down to the drawing-room at dinner-time, old Lady Scarlett, who used to give me half-crowns, and beg Frank not to thrash me, twenty years ago, told me that she was very glad to see me, and that she wanted to have a little quiet talk with me in the morning, and show me the new kitchen-garden. I am not a great hand at kitchen-gardening, and I never knew any one yet to promise you a quiet little talk unless there was something unpleasant to say. I thought I knew pretty well what she wanted, and was resigning myself to the prospect of a cross-examination upon Scarlett's doings in Japan, when George Elphinstone, who had been at school with Scarlett and with me, seized upon me as she released me, and said:

"You will tell me all about it to-night,

won't you, old chap? I never heard such a rum thing in my life."

" All about what?" said I.

" All about the Japanese lady," said he, as his wife took charge of him, and left me to wonder how Mrs. Potwin had become a subject of such widespread interest. I could understand that Lady Scarlett might have heard about the trip to Tokio and Nikko, or even that Frank might have written and told her that he contemplated marrying a Mrs. Nobody, of Nowhere. But I couldn't see how Elphinstone, or Tom or Dick or Harry, could be so well informed. I was not, however, left long in doubt. A dozen or so of people came into the room, most of whom I knew, and then there was the moment's wait which betokens that somebody has failed to heed the dressing-bell.

The door opened, and in walked Ysonde Potwin, gorgeously apparelled in a gown as nearly Japanese as a European gown can be. As soon as she had told Lady Scarlett that she hoped she was not too late, she came up to me and gave me both her

"IN WALKED YSONDE POTWIN"

hands, over which I fumbled helplessly. I know of nothing more distressing than to have a woman give you both her hands, unless it is to suddenly find that you are expected to kiss her hand.

"You didn't know I was here, did you?" she said. "I made Frank promise not to tell you." And then, dropping her voice a little, she added, "I haven't made up my mind whether I am going to marry him, but we are supposed to be regularly engaged, and everybody is just lovely to me."

I was told off to take her to dinner, and I do not mind confessing that I was exceedingly uncomfortable. I knew that every one in the house must think she was mad, and Scarlett more mad to think of marrying her. I felt sure that every one had heard her described as being a friend of mine. To say that in an English country-house Ysonde Potwin was absolutely impossible is putting it very mildly. She chattered like a magpie all through dinner, and it seemed to me that she made a deliberate effort to be as exotic as possible. I saw poor old Lady Scarlett drop her eyes

no one of them has ever shaken my belief
that an Englishman who is fortunate enough
to have the privilege of taking an English
gentleman's daughter for his wife is most
ill-advised if he marries an alien. But in
the case of Mrs. Potwin there was more
than this. I know that the American wom-
en who have made a footing in London—
and I don't for a moment mean to say that
it isn't a firm footing—would say, if they
were asked, that Mrs. Potwin was not as
they were. She was, however, quite pleased
with herself. She thought, as she told me
after dinner was over, that such a marriage
was just the surprising sort of thing that
would be likely to happen to her.

"I am so glad," she said, "to have you
to talk to. You see, all these people here
think I am regularly engaged to Frank. He
didn't want any one to know that it was only
a kind of an understanding ; but it is, just
the same. I have come over here to see
how I like living in England, just the same
as I went to Japan to see how I liked living
there. I think Frank is the kindest, most
good-natured man I ever saw, and if I didn't

think about anything but what was easy to do and pleasant to do, I'd make up my mind to marry him and have it over with. But if Temehichi is going to be a *shogun*, I think I ought to marry him, whether I want to or not. It's like having a chance to live in a fairy story. When I used to read about the little girl who married the prince made out of *nougat*, I used to vow I'd never marry an ordinary human being. And it seems like throwing away my only chance if I don't marry Temehichi. Most people never get a show to do anything so improbable."

"Is he making any headway with his revolution?" I asked.

"Oh, I suppose he is working at it all the time," she said. "I haven't had a letter from him for ever so long, and the last time he wrote to me he was perfectly furious. He called me Bad Woman and Gold Beak, and called Frank a dog, just the way he used to go on about poor Charley Hart. You see, he had heard all about my going to Nikko at the same time Frank was going there, and besides that, he was in an awful rage because I didn't go up to Yezo to see

some of his relations.   I thought if he was
in such a fury, I'd just let him walk up and
down till he cooled off, and so I came over
to England.   He said in his letter that he
was going to Japan, but I don't believe it,
and if he does he won't come here.   Anyhow, I don't want to talk about him any
more now.   While I was in Japan I was all
the while thinking about Japanese things,
and now I'm in England I want to think
about English things.   One thing I can't
make out is, why they don't dance in the
evening after dinner.   In America, when
there are a lot of people together in the
evening, they always dance.   There are four
or five couples here, anyway, and I think it
is the most ridiculous thing I ever saw with
that splendid wax floor not to make the
most of it.   But Frank says that somebody
who lives over on the other side of the river
is going to give a ball in two or three days,
and then I am going to dance until I can't
stand.   And now you had better go and
talk to somebody else.   I want to get better
acquainted with that girl with the white eye-
lashes over in the corner there, so I can tell

her to put something on them. She makes
me so nervous, the way she is now, I don't
know what to do."

And when Mrs. Potwin left me I saw
that the other men had already made their
way to the billiard-room, where I soon
found myself playing pool; and I had
no chance to talk with Scarlett that
night.

But it was easy enough to have all the
talk I wanted with his mother in the morning. She was very nice about it; I will say
that for her. She didn't abuse Mrs. Potwin. She was unhappy, and the more unhappy because she didn't know just how
unhappy she ought to be. I think that
Frank had perhaps been a little rough
about it. He didn't want to be asked a
lot of questions, which he would, indeed,
have been at a loss to answer, and, I fancy,
he had put his head down, like a bull at a
gate, and told his mother he wanted to
marry Mrs. Potwin, and would marry her,
whether anybody liked it or not. And now
the poor good creature had got me to cross-
question. The first thing she wished to

know was if Mrs. Potwin had ever been
connected with the stage. On this point I
was enabled to reassure her. Then she
asked if Mrs. Potwin was received by nice
people in California, and whether the nice
people in California *were* nice. As I don't
know three people in the whole State of
California by name, I felt justified in saying that there were very nice people in California, and that none of the Californians
who honored me with their friendship would
dream of making a wry face at Mrs. Potwin;
that she was very young, almost childish, indeed, and that it was highly probable that
some of her little eccentricities would dis-
appear in the course of a few years' quiet
life in England.

"Ah, if it were only that she is eccentric!" said Lady Scarlett. "One doesn't
mind that in the least. People may be
quite mad, for that matter. One of my
dearest friends firmly believes that Mary of
Modena ought to be on the throne, and
shakes her head every Sunday morning
when the prayers for the Queen and the
royal family are read. One quite under-

stands people being odd in that way; but—
I don't mind speaking to you very openly,
you are such an old friend of Frank's—I
think Mrs. Potwin is vulgar. I could ac-
custom myself to her; she isn't quarrel-
some; she isn't disagreeable; but I know
that, sooner or later, it will make Frank unhappy to feel that she isn't like other people. She is so young now, and all the
strange things she says are said in such a
graceful little way, that she seems like a
naughty child. And, I fancy, Frank likes
her all the better because she is different
from other people. Ten years from now,
when she has four or five children, it will
be dreadful to hear her talk as she does
to-day; and the worst of it is that the children will learn to say the same unheard-of
things that she does."

I tried my best to comfort the poor lady,
but she returned to the charge with an evident determination to know the worst and
have it over.

"Frank," she said, "has not seen fit to
talk very freely to me, but from something
which Mrs. Potwin herself said it seems that

it was not Mr. Potwin's death that took him from her."

I could not, of course, pronounce the fatal word "divorce" after she had dodged it so gracefully, but I gave her to understand, as delicately as I could, that the courts of the State of California not infrequently put asunder those whose joining together had proved inauspicious. And so Lady Scarlett knew the worst. She didn't ask why or how Mrs. Potwin's marriage had been broken. It was enough for her to know that it had been dissolved by process of law, and not by the death of one of the contracting parties. If her son was going to marry a divorced woman, she, at any rate, would try to do her duty by him, and by any one who bore his father's name. But I knew, as I left the old lady standing there among the bean-poles, that I had dealt her a cruel blow the day I first took her son to Ysonde Potwin's house in Yokohama.

VII

If the morning had been given up to
kitchen-gardening and remorse, the afternoon, at any rate, promised to be a pleasant
one. Mrs. Potwin was, naturally, having
very much her own way with Dunkin House
and its inmates, and it was her pleasure to
take possession of an old cedar-wood punt
that lay idly among the lily-pads. After
appointing herself captain of the lazy craft,
she ordained that Scarlett should serve for
crew and I for freight. She had selected
from among the mass of Japanese cushions
and draperies which he had brought from
Japan those which pleased her best, and
when she herself, dressed in a charming
little frock of Japanese silk, took her place
in the punt, her lap filled with apple blossoms, she looked like a stray leaf from a
Japanese picture-book dropped by some
persistent breeze upon the sober English
surface of the Thames. But she had not
proposed to herself an afternoon of summer
idleness, and I don't think I ever heard so

14

earnest a tone in her voice as when she told Scarlett to let the punt drift, and then said to me :

" I want to talk to you seriously. Sometimes you laugh at what I say and sometimes you scold me, but you always treat me as if I were a naughty little child who ought to be at school. But to-day I want to be serious, and I want you to help me decide and help Frank decide what he and I ought to do. If I were here alone with him, it would be no use for me to try to be wise. He just takes it for granted that everything is going to run smoothly, and that we are going to be married, and live happily ever after. Now will you listen to what I am going to say and tell me truly what you think ?"

I told her that I would do my best, and then she made Frank promise in his turn that he " would not take everything for granted."

" Well," began Mrs. Potwin, when she had assured herself an attentive hearing, " in the first place, I don't think it is right for me to go on being conditionally engaged

to Frank, and having all his friends think
it's a regular engagement. I told him before we left Japan that I didn't consider he
was any more held to it than I was, and
that he could back out whenever he wanted to. But he won't want to, because he is
obstinate, and even if he did want to he
wouldn't, because he'd be ashamed, and I
think we have got to make up our minds
about it one way or the other. In America
it is as easy as anything to break off an understanding like that, or even a regular engagement. I know lots of girls who have
been engaged five or six times, and they
don't think anything of it; but here in
England everybody seems to think it is a
very serious thing. It is just like getting
into one of your express trains. They lock
the doors of the car, and you have to stay
there until you get to where you have
bought your ticket for. If I go on staying
here with his mother and all his friends,
and then, afterwards, I tell him that I
don't think it is going to do, they will
all say I was a flirt and that I made a
fool of him, and he would hate that, be-

cause he is awfully proud. Wouldn't you, Frank ?"

" I don't like to look like a fool, if that's what you mean, my dear," said Scarlett. " But I don't see what you want to talk all this nonsense for. Of course we are going to be married sooner or later. I'm not hurrying you; I will give you all the time you want. It seems to me the simplest thing in the world. You and I had an awfully good time out in Japan together, and we have a good time here. Why shouldn't we be married and go on having a good time ?"

" I will tell you why," said Mrs. Potwin. " You know that man we saw the day we went over to Woodstock—the man who was driving what you call a piebald horse ? We call them *paint* horses in America. Well, I didn't see anything out of the way about it. I think a spotted horse is awfully pretty. But you and all the other men on the coach laughed at it, and said that the horse looked as if it came out of a circus. Well, now, I am like a spotted horse. I am very pretty, but I am not the correct thing in England.

Japan was a kind of a circus to you, and
when you saw me out there you thought
I was lovely; but if we got married, you
would find out, sooner or later, that all your
friends wondered why you harnessed up a
piebald horse instead of choosing a regular
every-day color like other people. I didn't
know it was going to be like that until
I came over to England. That is what I
wanted to come here for — to find out. It
isn't because I am a flirt; truly it isn't. I
haven't flirted with you the least bit, Frank.
I like you ever so much, and the only reason I don't want to marry you is, that I
don't believe it would work. Your mother's
awfully nice and kind to me, but I can see
that she doesn't think it is going to work
either. Do *you* think it would work?" said
the little woman, turning to me.

"I don't know what I think, my dear
Mrs. Potwin," I replied. "Sometimes I
fancy you are rather too feather-headed a
small person to marry anybody, but when
you talk like this you don't seem feather-
headed at all. I don't see that, after all,
it is anybody's business but yours and

Frank's, or that anybody else but you two can judge about it. If you both believe that you can be happy together, it is half the battle over already."

I felt rather a sneak as I said this, for, although I had been very careful not to express an opinion of any sort when I had been talking with Lady Scarlett that morning, I knew quite well that I had left her with the impression that I did not approve of her son's matrimonial project. But I was touched by what Mrs. Potwin said, and I was beginning to think that perhaps I had been unjust to her, and that she had more unselfishness and good feeling than I had given her credit for.

"If it is my turn now," said Scarlett, "perhaps I might say what I think, because, after all, I have something to do with it, you know. And what I've got to say is this: If the only reason you are afraid to marry me is that you think I will be ashamed of you, it's all rubbish. I am not a hand to be always arguing about things and talking politics and all that, and I know a great many people seem to think

I have no brains; but I know what I want as well as the next man—and what I want is you. I suppose what you are driving at is that if we had a house in town, and went up there every season, people would say I hadn't made a smart marriage. But what difference does that make to me? If I were a parson it might do me some good to marry a girl whose people were great swells and all that sort of thing. But I'm not. I don't want anything of anybody, and, as for being up in town and dining out every night, I hate all that. I like to be comfortable, and I think you and I would have the jolliest sort of a life together. If you have any real reason for thinking that we wouldn't, tell me what it is, but if it's only that you think you're a skewbald horse, I call it wasting time to talk about that."

"Well, that isn't all there is to it," said Mrs. Potwin, "but it all comes to the same thing"; then, turning to me, she said:

"Don't you think I ought to tell Frank about Temehichi? I have tried to tell him two or three times, but he won't let me."

"What's Temehichi?" said Scarlett.

"Some place in Japan where you were riding what you call a 'paint' horse in a circus? What do I care about that? Haven't I seen you often enough flying about Yokohama with no hat on, and wasn't I flying about with you, for that matter? I wouldn't want to go down Piccadilly that way, and I don't suppose you would either, and after we are married and settled I don't suppose either of us will want to do that sort of thing. And, as for your trying to tell me some story of yours, I know that one evening up in Nikko you wanted to tell me all about some man you had been engaged to, and I told you I didn't want to hear it. I know well enough you were married before, for that matter, and of course I wish you hadn't been; but I don't see any use in talking about it."

Mrs. Potwin asked me again if I didn't think she ought to tell Scarlett all about Temehichi, and in common honesty I had to say that I thought she ought.

And she did. There in the broad, square-shouldered punt, on the quiet, comfortable English river, she told him the whole story.

"ON THE QUIET, COMFORTABLE ENGLISH RIVER"

I knew, as soon as she began, that Scarlett
would not laugh at that. And when I saw
that she wasn't trying to tone it down at all,
that she meant to make him clearly understand that she had seriously thought of
marrying a little copper-colored servant-boy,
who was either a lunatic or worse—either
out of his head or engaged in some mad
scheme of getting up a twopenny-ha'penny
insurrection in Japan—I liked her better
than I had ever liked her before. Scarlett
heard her story to the end, leaning on his
long punt-pole, and from time to time
thoughtfully stirring the mud in the river-
bottom and watching the black clouds rise
through the clear water. When she had
said her say she looked up at him to see
how he was taking it, and I looked the other way. I wished more than ever that they
had not brought me with them. The punt
shot ahead vigorously, and we were half a
mile down the stream before Scarlett spoke.
Then, letting his pole drag idly through the
water, he said to Mrs. Potwin :

"I suppose you expect to have me tell
you what I think of all this, but I can't do

it yet.   You see, I am one of the slow kind
—so now we will talk about something else,
if you don't mind."   I saw in his face that
the story of Temchichi was gall to him.   A
moment later he let the punt run up to the
bank, and said :

"If you people will amuse each other for
a moment, there is a cottage just a hundred
yards from the shore that my agent's been
talking to me about, and I want to have a
look at it for myself."

It was as good an excuse as another, and
I could very well understand that he wanted
to be alone for a moment.   When we were
left there together in the punt, Mrs. Potwin
said, quietly enough :

"He sees now that I am a paint horse.
I guess, now that he knows about Temchichi, it will be easy enough to persuade him
that he had better not marry me.   Do you
know what I believe ?   I believe it was because Temehichi used to clean up the flat
that Frank thinks it is so awful.   It seems
just the same to him as if it were one of the
big footmen up at the house.   He doesn't
see the difference the least bit."

"It is a singular story, you know, when a man hears it for the first time," said I, a little sharply perhaps, for at the moment I felt much more sorry for Scarlett than for her.

"Oh, it's singular enough," replied Mrs. Potwin; "anybody would say that. But when you call it singular, that's a kind of a half-polite way of calling it disgusting. I supposed you'd be disgusted when I told you the story on board the steamer last year, only you didn't like me enough to care anything about it one way or the other; but it disgusts Frank; anybody can see that easy enough. There isn't any cottage up there. He's just gone off to cool down, that's all."

"That is quite likely," said I. "It can't flatter a man's vanity much to have Temehichi for a rival."

"It is so hard to make you Englishmen understand!" cried Mrs. Potwin. "With us, people's ideas are so different. You can't expect it to be any other way. There are a few people in New York and in Baltimore and one or two other big cities who

bring up their children on the English plan,
but a good many people laugh at them for it."

"And you were not brought up on the
English plan?" I asked.

"No," said Mrs. Potwin, "I wasn't. My
father was rich, and of course he had a
splendid position in Washington; but he
thought all those old-fashioned European
ideas were ridiculous, and I guess my mother thought so too. It's awfully hard to explain it, but if I could only make you understand, you wouldn't blame me half so
much. Why, you take it there in California: nearly all the old ladies whose husbands have so much money now—the old
ladies that everybody looks up to — they
worked with their hands thirty or forty
years ago. Maybe they weren't servants
in anybody else's houses, but they were
servants in their own houses, anyhow. They
worked like servants, they ate like servants,
they talked like servants, and they thought
like servants. According to our American
ideas they're commoner than the ladies in
the East, but I don't see but that it is just
the same everywhere. I have been up,

when I was a little girl, to stay with some cousins of mine in Vermont—people who were as proud as could be—but it was a farm, and the ladies used to do most of the cooking themselves. They had only one hired girl, and they used to have to get the men's dinner ready, hired men and all, and wait on them at table, too. Do you suppose that when a child sees such things, that child will grow up with English ideas about social distinctions and all that? Why, those old ladies up in Vermont would have thought any such talk as that worse than nonsense; they would have said it was downright wickedness. They had a kind of a Puritan idea that one person was just as good as another, and that it was wrong to be worldly, as they called it. That's the way all our grandmothers were in America. And we grow up to be as worldly as can be, and to want to spend lots of money, and to wear good clothes, and everything like that, but we still have their ideas about one person being just as good as another. I know I was wrong to encourage Temehichi to think about me, but if I had been in earnest it wouldn't have been wrong, according to the old American idea of things. You English people think it's awful bad manners for girls to flirt, in the joking kind of way our girls do, without trying to hide it; but I guess English girls brought up the way we are — girls in what you call the middle classes—are just the same. It isn't fair to judge me as if I had been brought up like your sisters. We don't have governesses tagging after us when we go out to walk: we go around alone, and of course we don't grow up so prim. It is very well for you Englishmen to be surprised at our American ways, but I have seen Australian girls come to America, and they carry on with everybody just as American girls do. They are not a bit more proud, and yet they are real English stock, aren't they? It isn't a mixture of Germans and Italians and French and everything else, as it is in America. They are all of them English enough, but Lady Scarlett would find their manners and everything else about them just as queer as anything I do."

" That may all very well be," said I, " but you must remember that the young ladies from Australia have not had just the sort of fathers and grandfathers that women like Lady Scarlett have had. They were English, if you please, but they were a very different sort of English, and a sort of English we don't know. A good many of their grandfathers were transported English convicts, and for that matter most of the men who go out to the colonies even nowadays are a worthless, shiftless lot, or else are the sons of worthless, shiftless people in England. If they were well off they'd stay at home. The emigration of the unfit is incidental to the survival of the fittest."

"Well," said Mrs. Potwin, " if you come down to that I suppose it was the same way with our grandfathers who went to America. If they hadn't been paupers or criminals or religious cranks like the Salvation Army or some other kind of no-account people they wouldn't have gone. And how can you expect me to have the same ideas that an English lady has when all her people have been taken care of like the gardens at

Dunkin House, for generation after generation?" And Mrs. Potwin, turning her head away, and nestling down in the cushions, added :

"I wish you would go and look at that cottage, too. I'm a little bit upset, and I'd like to be alone for a while." I stepped out of the punt, and as I walked up the green slope of the bank I heard her crying softly.

Scarlett was already far ahead of me, skirting the edge of a field of corn. No cottage was in sight. He had marched off, as Mrs. Potwin said, because he wanted to be alone. I was thoroughly uncomfortable. There was a wall at the farther end of the field, and when he came to it he put his elbows on it, and stood there with his hands crossed under his chin and his head bowed. As I came up behind him, I said :

"You had better come back to the punt, old chap. She feels just as bad as you do, and it's not very civil to leave her there all alone."

"Why didn't you stay with her, then?" asked Scarlett. "I wanted to be quiet for five minutes. I was afraid I might say

"IT WAS A GREAT BIRD'S HEAD, WITH GARNET EYES"

something I would be sorry for afterwards.
It's a beastly story—a beastly story."

It's not her fault that you didn't hear it
long ago," said I.

"Oh, you needn't make excuses for her,"
said Scarlett. "I'm not blaming her. She
doesn't look at things just the way you and
I do—that's all. It's filthy! That's what I
call it."

I made no reply, and we walked slowly
back across the field. As we neared the
river-bank I thought I saw the bushes move,
and wondered if Mrs. Potwin had left the
punt. But she was lying there, half hidden in the soft Japanese cushions. Scarlett
stepped into the punt, and, picking up his
pole, said:

"I fancy we'd better be making our way
up stream again, hadn't we?"

There was no answer, and, as I followed
him into the punt, I remarked that I had
gone to have a look at the cottage too. Still
there was no answer from Mrs. Potwin. I
leaned over the side of the punt to look at
her eyes and see if she were still crying, and
as I did so Scarlett looked, too.

Over her head, quite covering her face
and her yellow hair, and clasped tightly
around her throat, was a bronze helmet, a
larger copy of the one Temehichi had sent
her with the doll. It was a great bird's
head, with garnet eyes, and a beak like a
hawk's, made of gold. I thought at first
that it was a toy she had put on to make us
laugh.   It seemed an ill-timed farce, and I
had it on the end of my tongue to ask her
to take it off, when I saw something in the
position of her arms that made me reach
out to remove it myself. But it was clamped
on, shut like a trap with a strong spring.

I jumped out of the punt and up the
bank. Far away down the road I saw the
receding figure of a man, undersized, no
taller than a boy.

I turned to the punt again.   Scarlett was
holding her in his arms, the grotesque met-
al head, with its golden beak, hanging on
his breast.

He was picking at the joint in the side of
the helmet, and at last he found the spring
and lifted the casque from her shoulders.

Her yellow hair was matted by the weight

of the bronze, and a gray line encircled her
throat where the collar of the helmet had
compressed her soft flesh.   Her eyes were
staring, as the blue eyes of the wax doll had
stared.   And she was quite dead, suffocat-
ed by the monstrous thing that the Son of
Tokugawa had locked upon her head.

THE END